Wakefield Libraries
& Information Services

This book should be returned by the last date stamped above. You may renew the loan personally, by post or telephone for a further period if the book is not required by another reader.

RICHARD'S THINGS

Frederic Raphael

RICHARD'S THINGS

JONATHAN CAPE
THIRTY BEDFORD SQUARE LONDON

FIRST PUBLISHED 1973
© 1973 BY VOLATIC LTD

JONATHAN CAPE LTD
30 BEDFORD SQUARE, LONDON WCI

ISBN O 224 00952 4

PRINTED AND BOUND IN GREAT BRITAIN
BY RICHARD CLAY (THE CHAUCER PRESS) LTD
BUNGAY, SUFFOLK

FOR PAUL RAPHAEL

1

The miles were draining away. They were down to single figures when the traffic began to slow and thicken ahead of her. A new section of road was being constructed. She had driven with practised caution. Now she stopped behind a Volvo estate and eased her hands from the wheel. The wiper on the back window of the Volvo had cleaned a swathe in the caked dust. In spite of herself, she smiled. They had first seen a wiper on a back window when they were in Italy, she and Richard, on their way to Paestum. A Lancia Flaminia. They had been to see the villas at Ravello: eight years in June. They had laughed.

The new road was to be dual carriageway. Yellow levellers trundled over the site on fat wheels. Behind them, Constable trees wore their early green. A young man in a tartan shirt and cap posed with a red flag. The landscape shimmered, as if smoke were clearing. Ahead of Kate, to her right, where the road would bend on a new axis, stood a large oak; its branches spiked the morning from a dozen angles. There was no one near it. The young man with the flag turned to the line of motorists and nodded.

The oak disintegrated. The thick tree shuddered and burst open. Branches hung in the air for a second, as if on the wing with the hundreds of birds which jostled the sky, and then collapsed. The clap of the charge followed the execution. The ground shook.

The young man laughed and scratched his chest under his tartan shirt. A flag waved ahead and he gave an answering flourish. The traffic opened its slow concertina.

The car-park was large and empty. Kate stopped under businesslike buildings. The tarmac was marked with slanting slots. She stood shaking. Why had she left the Vitesse so far from the entrance? The air was colder than she expected. She was in the shadow of the curtainless buildings. She made herself move.

'I'm Mrs Morris,' she said. 'I'm looking for my husband.'

A cleaner was swabbing clean black-and-white vinyl tiles.

'He was brought in last night.'

'Your husband, you say?' The receptionist had a local accent. Her singsong exaggerated the interrogative. Kate imagined her to be mocking. 'I don't think you'll find him here. This is the maternity unit.'

The cleaner gave a gulping laugh and levered blackness from her squeegee into a blue plastic bucket.

Kate said, 'Then where will I?'

'Now was this an accident?' The receptionist became brisk. 'Your husband, you say?'

'They said Ipswich –'

'General Hospital, I expect, didn't they?'

'I asked a garage man and he said –'

'I'm afraid you're going to have to go back. You've overshot. You've overshot.'

Kate cocked her head. A baby was crying. She had no confidence that there were other people in the building. She wanted to go and find the child. She stood there, attentive, until the crying stopped.

'You're here,' the receptionist said.

'I beg your pardon?'

The woman had a leaflet giving details of emergency services. She twisted the inset map round on the dull, rubberized counter, to show Kate. 'You're here and you want to be here. What you've done is, you've overshot. If you go up to the main gate and turn left – do you know the town at all?'

'Coming from London,' the cleaner said.

'No,' Kate said. 'I don't. Not at all. But if you'll just show me once more.'

'You're wanting to get to here.'

'Thank you,' Kate said. 'You've been very kind.'

She bandaged her black-and-white woollen coat round her body and walked across the bubbly tiles to the glass door. An ambulance had arrived. A pale woman was being helped down the unfolded steps. Her face seemed as swollen as her body. Mugged by pregnancy, she appeared dazed and resentful. She might have been assaulted. The two women, the receptionist and the cleaner, looked at each other. 'London,' said the cleaner, 'the coat. You can tell. That's never local.'

2

Richard's plum-coloured Alvis was parked near the steps under the Palladian façade of the old hospital. Kate had been debarred by double yellow lines and forbidding signs from parking either in the forecourt or in the road. She had to find a place a few streets away and walk back along strict pavements past red regimented houses. Had Ipswich ever been a garrison town? The hospital had the guarded severity of a barracks. She went up to the Alvis, frowning. The boot was ajar. She swung it up. There was nothing inside except a flat webbing roll (Richard would borrow tools to work on the boat and forget to return them) and a few sheets of newspaper rustling with crumbs of earth. On the back seat of the car, together with an old floral cushion and some wrinkled tinfoil, were several rolls of plans. Richard was a landscape architect.

Kate leaned against the lustreless car for a moment and worked out the Roman date on the cornice above her. Then she had to go in. There was another receptionist; she was on the telephone and rolled her eyes in charitable suspicion as Kate approached. This hospital was dark. A light had to be kept burning by the switchboard. When Kate gave her name, she found she blurted it out as though she had made it up.

'I'm sorry?' said the receptionist.

'M,o,r,r,i,s. Morris.'

'Morris. Well, if you'd just like to sit down for a moment.'

She stood by a polished wooden seat under a noticeboard surly with warnings. There were 'Early Signs', they said, of a number of conditions. Prompt action alone might prevent serious consequences. Kate took a cigarette from her bag and put it to her dry lips. A Pakistani doctor smiled as he approached her. She feared she was supposed to recognize him. When he reached her, he wagged his finger and pointed to another notice: NO SMOKING. Kate jabbed her reddened cigarette back into the box; it split.

'Mrs Morris, I think I've found your husband. He's in Burton.'

'*Burton?*'

'Burton Ward,' the receptionist said, after allowing Kate a moment of panic. 'That's the Intensive Care. Now if you go down to the bottom of this corridor and then turn to the left and walk right the way through as far as you can go, you'll come to some stairs ... '

The hospital seemed to spread out like some tropical tree. The banyan? She walked and walked along narrow vaulted passages. Now and again drifts of sunlight lay banked against the walls. Elsewhere, Kate had to wince at the shadows. She walked and walked. An old gentleman, in a hairy dressing-gown with a tasselled cord he might have had since boarding school, came towards her, smiling. She stood aside, smiling in her turn, eager to read a genial omen into his greeting. She saw his smile reflected in that of a nurse who had entered the corridor behind her and realized that it was as impersonal as a freckle.

She saw Burton indicated and went up wide uncarpeted steps and through plastic doors into a new corridor. Stainless-steel wheelchairs were collapsed along one wall.

'How did it happen?'

'That I really don't know. What happened I can tell you, roughly. But how ... '

'I spoke to him yesterday. He said he was fine.'

'I'm afraid that's often the way. A man appears to be perfectly all right and –'

'I want to see him,' she said.

The doctor was younger than she. He had a beige face and evasive eyes. When he blinked, he blinked several times. Kate searched his face for comforting virtues: wisdom, energy, experience. She saw a young man who wanted a cigarette. He had taken her through into an empty corridor, she thought for privacy. Instead he was in a hurry to take out a packet of Guards and slap himself for matches.

'I want to see him,' Kate said.

'We shan't know anything for a day or so.' His name was Doctor Mace. He wore it like an advertisement on his white coat. He drew a few more puffs in the face of her impatience and then pinched out his cigarette and held the door for Kate. She thanked him.

3

A young girl was lying on the first bed. Her breasts were exposed. There were no blankets on the bed. Her breasts lolled in two uneven lumps on either side of her chest. She had broad nipples. A nurse came and drew the sheet up over the unconscious girl and covered her breasts, as if they had died. Then she sat down by the bed and slapped the girl's wrists.

'Come along, Brenda,' she said. 'Come along now. It's time to wake up. Come along.'

The girl pouted in her self-induced sleep. A sly band of white showed under her eyelids. Her unconsciousness might have been a joke.

'We've been helping him breathe,' Mace said.

Richard was lying in another of the high, stiff beds. He too was covered with a sheet. It looked tidy, but she went and arranged it. She wanted her arrival to mean that now they could get busy. She wanted them to have been waiting for her.

'Darling, it's me. It's Kate.'

The tube in his nose seemed to irritate him. She expected him to sneeze. His face puckered and re-lapsed. His hands were white and lay palms up. A needle on the respirator twitched, fell back and twitched again. Kate consulted the doctor's face, but it gave no reading. He looked at his watch. The respirator twitched regularly.

'Sister, I wonder if we could find Mrs Morris a cup of tea?'

Kate held the hand nearer to her. 'Is he asleep?'

'He's in a state of unconsciousness. Quite to be ex-pected in the circumstances.'

'Are you a Scotsman?' Kate said.

'Irish; Belfast. But I lived in Scotland as a boy. And I did my training in Edinburgh.'

'Doctor Mace, how long is this likely to go on, this stage?'

'Come along now, Brenda, time to wake up.' Be-yond the pretty curtains, the nurse was working on the girl. 'Brenda, you've slept long enough now. Wake up now.'

'It's virtually impossible to say,' the doctor said.

'Weeks?' Kate said. Her eye was caught by a plump paper sack in the corner of the cubicle. It was fast-ened by staples and there was a label on it: Richard Morris.

'Your husband's things,' Mace said.

'Yes, of course,' Kate said. 'Doctor Mace, how did my husband get here?'

'How did he get here?'

'He wouldn't have been able to drive, would he?'

'I doubt that. I doubt that. I should have to make inquiries. I wasn't here myself.'

'Somebody must have driven him.'

'I would assume an ambulance.'

Kate found she had her tea. She said, 'Doctor Mace, forgive me, but – we do have – we are on this scheme. Boopa. I mean, if there's anyone in London who could do anything –'

'The consultant here has seen him,' Mace said. 'And he'll be coming back later. Quite honestly, there isn't much that anyone can do at this stage.'

Kate said, 'I don't think I understand –'

'Recovery in these cases is slow and it depends largely on the patient. All we can do is take care of him and –'

From beyond the pretty curtain came a blurted, wordless cry. The cry was repeated, louder, as if the first one had been a rehearsal: a shameless, almost threatening groan. Brenda was coming back to life.

'I must go,' Mace said. 'If there's anything you want, please ask Sister. Will you be all right?'

'I shall be all right,' Kate said. 'Sister, I wonder, should I bring him some pyjamas? I expect the rest of my husband's things are at the hotel. I hate to see him –'

'It's not necessary,' the Sister said. 'We prefer to nurse them naked.'

A tube ran from under Richard's sheet into a yellow bottle.

'Twenty-four hours ago,' Kate said.

The sister took Richard's pulse. The other woman's eyes measured Kate as she exercised her right to her husband. Kate sat down by the bed, next to the brown paper sack. When the Sister had gone, she made herself speak. 'I think I shall have to go soon and see about a room. I shall have to find somewhere to sleep.' He sighed a few seconds later. He strained and fell back under the heavy bond of his flesh. She said, 'I shall come back later. I shall tell them where I am. I shan't be far.' She said these firm, unfamiliar things as though she had never said anything else, or spoken any differently. 'I shall be back soon.'

She knew no one in the town. Richard had come to see a client who lived down the estuary, towards Harwich. The man owned an estate which he proposed to turn into a country club and marina. He had commissioned a survey and had agreed to go ahead with a more detailed scheme, but to Kate he was no more than a name in the diary. If she told him what had happened, he would say, 'Good heavens, I am sorry.' She would have to find where Richard had been staying. Perhaps she could have his room. He had been booked for two nights.

She left the hospital after the evening shift. She had waited to meet the Night Sister. She was a blonde Australian with a fob watch pinned above her left breast. She wore flat, squashy shoes. They gave her a thick efficient stride. Kate hoped that she would be asked to stay, but the ward was not tuned to visitors. She knew herself unwanted.

The Alvis was still there. She slammed the boot. This time it caught. A clergyman drove in through the glistening black gates and parked his Morris Traveller where it said MEDICAL STAFF ONLY. She did not return his greeting at first, but then she called out, 'Oh good evening,' when he was halfway up the steps.

4

The hotel was called the Orwell. It was in a new, brick section of the town among offices and supermarkets and insurance buildings. It wore the badge of a large company. It looked empty from outside, but the cocktail lounge was full of people in low chairs, leaning towards each other with faceless intimacy and murmuring 'our people' and 'your people'. Signs in London lettering indicated the way to the Suffolk Snuggery and the Orwell Room. Kate asked for the manager. Mr Ritchie, they told her his name was. When he arrived, he was dark and young and Italian: Mr Ricci.

'I am so sorry about your husband. How is he to-night?' He was putting on a midnight-blue dinner-jacket over his ruffed evening shirt as he spoke. An evening smile slipped over his face at the same time.

'He's no different,' Kate said. 'I wonder if you could tell me, was it you who took him in to the hospital by any chance?'

'No, it was not I personally.' He would have liked to give her all his attention but he had to keep an eye on his staff. He was prompt to call out a room number when the desk clerk hesitated before a pair of Japanese businessmen who had repeated it over and over in their perfect, incomprehensible English.

'I wonder if you know what's been done with my husband's luggage. Is it still by any chance – ?'

'We find that out for you, Mrs Morris, right away.'

'And I shall need a room, if – '

'Of course. We arrange something. Jean-Pierre, fais demander où se trouve la valise de Monsieur Morris qui avait soixante-sept hier soir. Don't worry, Mrs Morris. We will arrange something.'

'Who would know exactly what happened?'

The manager shrugged in sympathetic adjournment.

After a conference with the desk clerk, a room was cleared for Kate. A boy showed her up. No sound came through the double-glazed windows. She could see the station and the football ground and the thin, deep wound of the river. She could not believe that the room was different from any other. Twin beds; the TV; a desk; a wastepaper basket; a pendent phone without a dial; an uneven reproduction of a Riviera scene. She was hungry, but without appetite.

An aproned black man brought Richard's case. The key was attached to the handle. Richard was not good at locking things. Pyjamas; razor; clean shirt; socks. Books, he always took books: *The New France*; *New Lives, New Landscapes*; everything new! Catalogues; sketch-books; a tape-measure; the diary. A bent paperback: *Underground with the Oriole*. Kate opened that.

She could not sit down to eat in the hotel. She looked out for a pub where she might find a sandwich, but there was none near. The hotel bar sold only crisps. In the end, she bought two bars of Kit-Kat at a confectioners' on her way back to the hospital.

'He's breathing a bit easier this evening, your husband.' The nurse was Jamaican.

'You really think so?' Kate said. 'I thought so too, but – '

'Definitely, definitely. He talked to me.'

'He talked to you. Are you sure? My husband?'

'Oh wait a minute, wait a minute. No, it was somebody else. It was Mr Leaf. I talk to him, but he not talk to me, not yet. He will though.'

Kate sat again by the paper sack and wished the nurse out of the cubicle. She took Richard's hand and turned it over and read the blank of his palm. 'It's me again,' she said. 'Just like I said.' His eyelids, his eyelids seemed to lift. 'Oh my God,' Kate said. She wanted to call somebody. His hand felt round hers. She flung herself down with her face against him. 'Oh yes, darling, it's me. It's Kate. Kate's here.' Now she wanted the nurse back again, but the medicine trolley had come in. They were checking night doses with the superintendent. 'I've got a room, so I'm all right. Nothing to worry about. I'll be here as long as you are.'

He opened his eyes. His lips shaped a word that he tried to squeeze out beside the tube from the respirator. She leaned down towards him again.

'What, darling? What?'

Richard pushed the word out like a kiss. 'Shit!' His

18

eyes watched her slyly. She let out a blurt of laughter and pressed his hand against her breast. He closed his eyes again.

She heard the intrusive rattle of Sister drawing the curtains open next door. 'How are we this evening?'

'All right. Not bad. You know.' Brenda might have had a bad cold. 'Considering.'

'They'll be coming to take you home tomorrow, if you behave yourself.'

'I thought me mother might have come in to see me. That's never raining, is it?' Was this the girl who had given those two brutal cries? 'I suppose if I'm all right to go tomorrow.'

'You will be,' Sister said. 'It's home for you tomorrow. And don't bother to come back,' she whispered as she came through to Kate. 'If there's one thing I can't stand, it's these girls. Sometimes I could . . .'

'He said something,' Kate said. 'He woke up and said something.'

'Did he now? And what was that, pray?'

'Oh . . . ' Kate shook her head. 'The thing is, he definitely said something. Which must mean – '

'It's certainly progress. And we don't want to stand in the way of progress, do we?'

A patient was being wheeled in from the operating theatre. Sister went to hold open the breeze doors while three nurses shunted the trolley. The patient was still unconscious. A Chinese nurse was holding up a bottle of plasma drip.

Richard said, 'Where's – ? Where's – ?'

Kate said, 'Who, darling? Bill? Bill's at school.'

'Ah! And – '

'And he'll come and see you at the weekend. He

wanted to come, but I said no. It's such a way. I thought I'd better see how you were first. You're much better already. I shall be talking to him later tonight. Anyway, he's fine. You're the idiot.'

He considered her for a long time and then he said, 'I'm sorry. I'm so sorry.'

She leaned her head down and lay with his palm against her cheek. The three nurses were trying to move an empty bed from the cubicle opposite before sliding the trolley into its place. There was not much space and they obstructed each other. One of the castors on the empty bed went over the Jamaican's toe. She began to giggle. The others frowned; until they began to giggle too. The Chinese nurse was in contortions. She pitched and buckled with the tide of laughter. And all the time, she worked to keep the frosted bottle above her head. The sheets on the trolley were stabbed here and there with dots of blood. Amid their giggles, the nurses extracted the empty bed and pushed the trolley into position. As soon as the plasma bottle had been hooked into place and the Chinese nurse was free to giggle without danger to her patient, she relapsed into solemnity.

Sister said, 'Mrs Morris, I think you should be going soon.'

It was twenty past nine.

Kate said, 'Sister, I wondered – would you like me to take that away? Richard's things.'

'It's doing no harm where it is, unless you want to.' The Sister looked at the man in the bed.

'He did seem quite a lot better,' Kate said. The Australian said nothing. She held Richard's wrist for a second and then went away on her squashy soles.

5

Kate spoke to her son, Bill, from the hotel soon after ten. He was at a co-educational boarding school in Hampshire. He sounded calm and comforting; Kate, though calm, was not comforted. She recognized a sort of patience in his voice. He was being reliable, and she saw it as a wish, an assumption. She was grateful to be able to rely on him; she hated the tone.

She went to the desk for her key.

'Sixty-seven, please.'

The clerk went straight for it. She was relieved; she felt she was in a foreign country where her few words had luckily been understood. When the man came back with the key, he asked her to sign the register. It was a heavy, deckle-edged book. While she signed, a businessman came for his key. From the direction of the Orwell Room came the blur of dated music. While the businessman told the clerk Yes, he'd had a surprisingly good day all in all, remarkably good actually, Kate rolled back the pages, savouring random names. Mr and Mrs Richard Morris had arrived the previous day.

She nodded at the jagged signature (Richard's pen had snagged on the thick paper) and then she closed the register and swivelled it to the clerk. She must have stood there for a second or two, with a goodnight smile on her lips. The businessman was in his thirties, tall and polished with a drink or two. He was handsome and his invitation had an unambiguous candour.

'Would you care to come and have a drink? I really have had a hell of a good day and here I am all by myself. I wish you would. Just for the hell of it. If you're alone and ... '

She believed she would accept. She saw herself on a mirrored pillar and believed she recognized a woman who would say yes. 'No, thank you, so much,' she said, 'but I really won't.'

'Do,' he said. He would tell her things about his wife and his children, he might even show her a photograph with a bent corner, and he would ask nothing of her that she was not willing to offer. He was a nice man; his bruised charm promised that he would not be what she thought he was, certainly not unless she wanted him to be.

'Truly,' she said, and turned towards the lift. She stumbled and felt him prompt at her elbow.

'I wish you would.' His voice was bold and gentle. He would confide in her how much he liked women and how rarely he had a chance to have a serious talk with one. He would agree with her that the worst thing about marriage was that one never had a chance to talk to other women seriously, as women. He would tell her that he was very happy with his wife and that the worst thing about his job was that he had to be away so much. He would ask her about herself and she would tell him nothing, because, she would say, there was nothing to tell.

'You're very kind,' she said. 'But I honestly won't.'

The lift was small. She huddled in the corner away from the doors he had closed behind her. She was not surprised that she had refused him. When had she been surprised? Only at pleasure that she remembered; she remembered once when Richard lifted her and entered her before she was ready, before she could imagine he would, and she had cried out at the sudden scandal of pleasure. She braced herself in the corner of the lift with the doors shut, pushing with her feet against the floor, her shoulders in the hard angle behind her. Pleasure had always taken her by surprise.

The door of the lift opened. It was the businessman. She had not pressed the button. The lift had not moved. She straightened and stood helpless.

'Good heavens, I'm terribly sorry. I thought it had already gone and come back.'

'I thought I was moving and all the time I wasn't.'

'I decided to go up myself. Nothing left to do but watch the box. Unfortunately.'

'No,' she said. She accompanied him to the fifth floor (he assumed that she was going higher) and then she pressed the button for the ground again.

Ricci had been dancing. Kate sat in the cocktail lounge over a large, unwanted scotch. Local people in elderly dresses and chapped dinner-jackets had come out of the Orwell Room and were chatting in the cool. Ricci was shaking hands with a one-armed man whose wife's patient frown promised a lifetime of implacable docility. Ricci had already seen Kate. He was using her to be free of the old couple. She smiled into her glass as he shook hands once again, with fugitive sincerity. 'You can do it any time you want, Colonel, that's a promise. I'm quite serious. Quite serious. Now you must excuse me. But please, don't forget, because . . .'

'I shall hold you to that,' the Colonel said. Suspicion was screwed into his eye like a monocle.

Kate said, 'Mr Ricci – '

'Oh, Mrs Morris.'

'Mr Ricci, I hate to bother you. Please sit down.'

'I've been doing a reel,' Ricci said. 'I should like to sit down. I have done many things, but a reel . . . '

'Mr Ricci, the person my husband was with – '

'I'm sorry, Mrs Morris. Forgive me. Yes.'

'It's perfectly all right. The person my husband was with, when he arrived. I know all about it; it's perfectly all right. The young lady. Will you have a drink?'

'No, no, thank you, I'm . . . She left. She left this morning. Naturally, I assumed – '

'Naturally. I knew that much, of course,' Kate said, 'but how? By train?'

'I assume. I don't – '

'I take it it was she who drove my husband to the hospital?'

'As I say, I don't – I can't be sure. I rather think there was an ambulance called.'

'It's perfectly all right, Mr Ricci,' Kate said. 'Just so long as I know.'

6

She allowed the bath to grow cold around her. She had pulled the television into the door of the bathroom. The sound hurt her. She turned it down. The people mouthed. She did not care what they said or what they did; their movements promised that the journey was passing. She was flat in the bath. She had never had large breasts. Her belly fell below the level of her hips. The skin was puckered below her navel; Bill, and Erica. She had soaped herself as if for a stranger, or an operation. The bubbles had burst now; phantoms of grease floated on the stretched water. She was flat: without volume or energy. When the phone purled, she shook her head: no, she would not take it, no. No, she shook her head. She would not unsheathe herself from the dull sleeve of water. She had no strength. She let the wall-grip draw her up. She tottered on high naked heels, handed across the room by the thoughtless arms of the furniture. She fell naked and wet across the candlewick bed. No, she prayed, no. And then politely, 'Yes?'

She went out of the hotel in a sort of wild rage. The sound of music came, architecturally muted, from the Orwell Room. There was no brutal response to her brutal need. She fell into the tepid bath of a provincial night. They had been tactful on the telephone, as if death were a temporary crisis; they had mentioned it with a host of other symptoms: 'a massive attack, cardiac collapse . . . ' They had done everything they could.

She wanted to see him. She saw him. He was not there. She searched for him in his emptiness. He had gone. They brought her tea and she hated them because there was only one cup. She wanted another cup to be his, and to sit there cooling, untasted only because he chose not to taste it. She hammered on the empty door where he should be. She burst in, like a

25

rescuer too late to a house consumed by cold fire. She climbed the little ladder to the attic, where cold flames sizzled and crackled among the joists. She shuddered at freezing burns and stumbled among ferns of frost that scorched her face. Where was he? It was a desertion. He had left her. They said it was wrong for her to stay. She looked at them with defenceless slyness. He had made plans. She would not be sentenced to that place where tea was the only medicine. It was not all over. He had made plans for her to join him. He was waiting in some secret place where reservations had been made for the two of them: Mr and Mrs Richard Morris.

'You've had a bit of a sleep, that's good.'

'What have you done with him? You haven't moved him.'

'Are you sure you wouldn't like us to give you something?'

'Where is he?'

'Another cup of tea?'

'Because I don't want you to do anything.'

'You should go home, Mrs Morris.'

'I'm going to go home,' Kate said. 'I'm going to go home.'

'I think you should let us find somebody to go with you.'

'Somebody?'

'To go with you. You shouldn't go on your own.'

Kate said, 'I've got two cars here already. We've already got two cars here. I don't want anybody. I don't want anybody at all. I shall be fine.'

7

The boy in the tartan shirt was waving a green flag this time. In the field, a tractor team was threading chains under the gnarled wooden tooth which was all that remained of the oak tree. Kate drove steadily. She would have been glad to drive all day.

She had to stop for petrol. She turned off the engine and waited. A man came up to her window. He seemed very large. She shied from him, but even then she could not take him in. He was huge.

His voice said, 'Sorry, none of my business, but you do know this is a self-service, don't you?'

Kate said, 'I didn't. Thank you.'

'Sad but true. No nice men to put it in for you these days. You have to put it in yourself.'

She got out of the car. 'Of course. Silly.' She looked at the pump, the levers and indicators. How did one help oneself?

'Allow me. Ninety-nine be all right for you?'

She said, 'Ninety-nine? I want six gallons.' Incomprehension made her precise. 'Not more than six.'

'Of the ninety-nine.'

'I'm sure I can manage.'

'My pleasure,' said the man. She noticed his coat, a tweed tent, but she still could not see his face. She was locked; she could not raise her head to look at his face. He was talking to her as the figures spun on the pump face. 'Let me guess now.'

Kate said, 'Guess?'

'You're on your way to London, right so far? Right. You've ditched the old man and you're free. You're on the lam, right?'

'On the lamb?'

'On your own. No responsibilities. Free to enjoy yourself. Do as you please and hang the expense. Six gallons. Date with a girl friend, I'll bet you.'

'Who do I pay?' Kate said.

'You pay inside. They won't come out even in the fine weather now, but there's always someone to take your money; you can rely on that. If it is a girl friend of course. Well, am I right?'

'Will he know how much or . . . ?'

'He'll know. I'm right about you being married anyway, aren't I? Must be!'

'No,' she said. 'Actually. No, I'm not.'

'I'd have lain anything,' the man said.

She came out of the office with a flat snake of trading stamps. If she had had two more gallons, she would have been entitled to a French wineglass.

So long as she recognized nothing, she was content, she was normal. She returned smiles, where they were given, and shared impatience, when other drivers were impatient. She was powerless against her competence. She drove home without incident: London, Putney, Kingston bridge, home. She saw herself arrive and unlatch the white wooden gate of 14, Oxford Road, and put the car in the drive. She saw herself at the front door with her key. No one would notice that anything whatever had happened so long as she gave them no cause to suspect. She was like a spy; the ordinary was her disguise. She mimed banality and, for the moment, restored it. She put her bag on the hall table with the rickety leg. She looked round this house in which she had lived for fourteen years and it was so strange that she felt perfectly at home.

She wanted to keep it a secret. If no one knew, it was not true. Her only spell was to be silent. She resisted death by refusing to acknowledge it. She held out like a seller. It was her joke against God. She did not believe in God, except to hate Him. She would not accept His price. Her hatred was decorous. She gave no rough symptom of it. Politeness was always her weapon. Whatever she disliked she had always treated with special courtesy. She was in the house as she had been in it the morning he left it. When she considered it, she was calmer now than she had been then, and less deserted. For at least several hours, she would live in the past. She had heard nothing of his illness. He would come back.

She took inventory of the room in which she was sitting. She sat and waited for pain. Meanwhile she was in a suburban drawing-room. She was looking out across the long room, through the tall Victorian bay window on to the roses. They had not bloomed yet. The buds were sweet for the ants.

The house was too large to have been expensive. Richard had put in the heating himself. They had painted it together. It had belonged to a dentist. She was sitting in the old waiting-room. There was an ornate mantelpiece, curious with cubbyholes. The oar Richard had won in his college boat was hanging on the short wall behind her. It was reflected in the mirror ensconced in the wood of the mantelpiece. She did not understand reflections, but there it was.

29

She wanted the pain to return. She waited, it must have been a full hour, and then she went into the kitchen. Richard's boat was on chocks in the garden, one side repainted, the other not. She came in and drank milk from a topless bottle, wishing for sourness; it was sweet. She ate bread and Marmite and finished a lolling jelly from the fridge.

8

Peter Workman was forty-two, a year older than Richard. He wore the uncreased face of a habitual joker disconcerted into solemnity. She wondered, seeing him on his way to the car, how he would manage on his own. As he came towards her, he stumbled and stamped to recover his balance. She saw the stumble as elephantine tact. He would have hurt himself if he could. He had been in the boat with Richard. His name was on the blade of the red oar above the picture rail: Number 2.

'There's absolutely nothing one can say, is there?'

He sat in the car beside her. She told him everything, taking a dull pride in the flatness of her account. He might have been a policeman who had heard nothing with which he did not sympathize and nothing on which he could act. 'At least,' he said, 'at least – at least he didn't, well, feel anything. I know it isn't much consolation.'

'None,' she said, and smiled at him, as if grateful that, whatever he could do, he could not console her.

They were sitting in the gravel yard in front of the office. Richard and Peter had been lucky. They had joined forces early enough to have pleasant premises. The offices were in an old boat-builder's yard, a wooden building so impregnated with varnish that Peter used to say that they could never employ anyone who smoked. 'One match and whoomf, up she goes!' The nurseries, which he had inherited from a bachelor uncle, were further down the river, beyond Teddington: six and a half acres. They had once been in the middle of open country; they were now surrounded with houses. They could be reached more easily by water than by road. Richard had tried to persuade their accountant to let him run his boat on the firm.

During the first four years of his marriage, Richard had worked with a London architect. 'I must have measured most of the nicest buildings ever converted into offices and guzzle shops,' he told Peter Workman at the boat club reunion where they had met again. Peter recognized Richard's discontent and he was quick to be generous; it was almost a kind of greed. He wanted to expand his business and Richard was keen to get out of London. Peter offered a fifty-fifty partnership. Who could complain? Peter worked hard; Kate could hardly expect him to make Richard the senior partner, but at times, when she was doing the books and saw the figures, she thought of Richard as a victim. Peter did not fail to be appreciative. 'I'm just a shit-shifter compared to old Dick,' he would say. 'Dull old brawn to bright old brain.' Kate thought he was not really so modest. He had made a good bargain. There was a certain cunning in his geniality.

He sat there with her in the car and she knew what an effort of imagination it needed in him to be so commonplace. Sympathy sat on him like a bully. It was against his nature to endure a situation about which no joke could be made. Sooner or later, he would try to make her laugh.

Two of the men were loading polythene-sheathed trees into the van. Peter watched them out of the corner of his eye, hoping to catch them in some efficient frivolity so that he could prove himself the friendly officer. When the girl came out of the office, Kate knew at once who she was. She carried a tartan tote bag. Her jeans were too short for her. She wore no socks.

'Who's that?' Kate said.

'That, oh that's Marie-José.'

'Ah.'

'You've met her, haven't you?'

'Have I?'

'Surely. She's been with us for some time now.'

'What's she like?'

'She's not too bad at all. Quite useful. Has been anyway. She's leaving actually, unfortunately.'

'Oh? Why?'

'She's French. I'm sure you've met her. Oh you know what these girls are like.'

'Where's she going?'

'That I don't know. Moving on. They all do. You can't keep anybody any more – '

'Marie-José what?'

'Clavand. Clavand.'

'She doesn't look very well. Has she been ill?'

'She may have. I don't see that much of her. I believe she has the last couple of days. She's quite capable. Bit of a scruff but – '

'Does she live nearby?'

'That I don't know. That I can't tell you.'

'She worked with Richard, I presume?'

'Well, more in his department than mine, let's say. You know me, Kate, I'm just basically a man who shifts assorted flora from one place to another. Richard does the thinking.'

'Did,' Kate said.

He put his arm round her then, in its leather-patched sleeve.

'Oh fuck it all,' he said. 'Kate, I – '

'You don't know what to say. Don't say anything. There's no need for you to. How long has she worked here?'

'I'm sure she brought some things up to your house. She brought the books over on one occasion, I'm sure she did. She's been with us about, oh, five, six months.'

'It's possible. Or it's possible that I wasn't there.'

'They none of them last these days.'

'Would you say she was pretty?'

'I wouldn't say pretty.'

'Attractive?'

'She's French,' Peter Workman said. 'I don't really know much about her. Yes, I suppose she's averagely attractive. I've never thought about it, quite honestly.'

Kate said, 'Someone'll have her address, will they?'

'Presumably they must somewhere. In case there's anything that has to be forwarded.'

The girl had collected her bicycle from the shed.

Kate watched her as she wheeled it out of the gate. The girl seemed unaware, as she pedalled along behind the hedge and disappeared, that there was anyone in the world who wished her harm.

9

Kate was wonderful. The family saw courage in a dignity which was sustained by hatred. Throughout the service and the long walk in the sunshine to the fresh grave, under the steep, shrill noise of the jets, Kate was buoyed up by the mounting thrill of her purpose. As she followed the coffin to the grave, she thought only of the girl. The supporting hands which reached out, from her mother, from Peter and Margaret Workman, were intrusions from which she was sharp to sever herself. Bill did not touch her. He stood close by her, taller than his personality. He was sixteen and he had grown bigger than she. Yet she looked down for him. His treason was that he was big enough to be separate.

There were cars to take them back to Oxford Road. Peter Workman was the organizer. He ran about; he made mild jokes with the drivers; he dragooned the older generation. He made himself useful. Margaret Workman had looked after the food. Everything was ready when they returned to the house. There were sandwiches and cakes from the little Frenchman in the High Street.

Margaret had to leave before the last of the guests; Peter stayed on. He and Bill carried dishes and cups out of the sitting-room. As they left, people embraced Kate and made her promise them things. They held her by the upper arms and looked into her eyes. They searched her for 'silly' symptoms. Soon only close family was left. Kate could hear her mother talking in the sitting-room. She went into the kitchen. Her mother's big beige labrador, Bertie, slid out to join her. She fed him scraps, glad of eyes that demanded something she could give.

The kitchen had a sloping roof. Richard had renovated it. A couple of the men had put in the new glass and timber frame. The cupboards he had built himself. The old kitchen had been dark and cold. The new one, with its liver-coloured quarry tiles and its generous windows, was warm and sunny. But the original kitchen, in spite of the antique stains and the splintery floor, had been her own territory.

Bill came in, carrying a tilted tower of cups. She watched him with a mixture of sympathy and malice. She wanted to see the cups reach the basin safely; she also wanted them to topple. Peter followed, with unused cakes.

'Where shall I bung these?'

'Oh Peter, you are sweet, you really needn't. There's a bin under the sink, or there should be.'

'It seems a pity.'

'Take the uneaten ones home with you, I wish you would. I can't exactly see myself sitting here eating up cakes in the next little while.'

'I'll take them,' Bill said. 'You know, if no one else wants them.'

35

Peter said, 'You don't row, do you, at your place?'

'Who, us?' Bill said, when no one else could have been intended. 'All pull together, you mean? No, we don't, I'm afraid. We're not unduly organized in that respect.'

'I enjoyed it,' Peter said.

'It's probably rather enjoyable, but we happen not to do it.'

'What sports do you do actually?'

'I like badminton,' Bill said. 'I used to like soccer.'

They might have been meeting for the first time. Peter had known Bill since he was four years old. Kate went into the sitting-room where her mother was plumping cushions and talking to Richard's father.

'You never met my other son,' Mr Morris said, 'did you? Bruce?'

Mrs Sells smacked a braided cushion soundly. 'If I did, it was a long time ago.'

'Please leave that.'

'They've been out in Caracas,' Mr Morris said.

Mrs Sells had had an antique business since the death of her husband. Kate's father had been drowned. He had fallen into not very deep water while releasing his boat from a buoy. He was wearing heavy boots and although a good swimmer he had been too encumbered to save himself. His wife had been a lady of leisure, as she said rather too often, until his death. She had then shown remarkable energy. While selling some of the furniture (it had been her intention to move into a smaller house), she discovered that she had a gift for business. She bought as well as sold and never left Stiles, the double-gabled house, near Farnham, where she had lived with her husband. She no longer made a distinction between friends and clients. She had had little aptitude for intimacy; she had come to discover the pleasures of formality. She had grown younger and stronger. She could move sizeable pieces of furniture single-handed. She specialized in oak. Every time Kate and Richard ate in her house, they ate from a different, and longer, table. She travelled and bought widely, yet she seemed always to be at Stiles. Richard said she travelled by broomstick.

'You know that's a very nice table you found that time,' Mrs Sells said.

'I'm not selling,' Kate said.

'I was admiring it.'

'I know what you were doing,' Kate said. 'You needn't do that either. Leave things where they are. My Mrs Jenkins'll be in in the morning.'

'You sit down,' Mrs Sells said. 'What you need is a stiff drink.'

'Mummy, Bill ought to get back to school. You couldn't drop him on your way possibly, could you?'

'Have him here for a few days, why don't you? No one'll mind.'

'He did offer, but he's better with his friends.'

'Then let me stay,' Mrs Sells said. She looked older as she spoke. 'Mrs Thing's perfectly all right. She's used to coping. And she knows where I am. Lionel'll be back after the weekend.'

'I'd truly sooner you took Bill.'

'I was only offering,' Mrs Sells said.

'I know,' Kate said.

37

10

'Why do I hate everybody so much?'

'Do you?'

'I'm afraid I do. Everyone's been as nice as they know how and all I can do is hate them. I'm really very ashamed.'

'Me included?' Peter Workman said.

'I couldn't have done without you,' Kate said. 'Then you always were the one for the disagreeable jobs.'

'They're the only ones I can do,' Peter said. 'You know that.'

'He's dead,' Kate said. 'Peter, he's dead.'

'I know,' Peter said. 'It's a bastard. It's a real bastard. If only there was something one could do.'

'Yes,' Kate said.

'At least one thing: there's quite a bit in the kitty; I mean Dick's share of the biz, if you feel like selling up. Obviously it's up to you, but ... at least there's that. If you want to realize on it, you're perfectly entitled, God knows.'

'I'll do whatever you want me to do,' Kate said.

'No, the thing is, the ground's worth quite a decent amount,' Peter said, 'and with planning permission, which is highly likely, well ... '

'We can all go and live in the South of France,' Kate said.

'One is a bit tempted,' Peter said. 'Of course, money's not the only consideration, but ... Oh dammit, Kate, this isn't what I want to talk about at all. I'm sorry. What the hell does it all matter? It's really absurd.'

They might have been quarrelling. He was hot and abrupt. They stopped where a bar of the tow-path railing had been bent in a shallow U; Peter put his foot up. A couple of boys and a girl, in jeans and fringed jackets, were wheeling bicycles across the girder bridge above the weir. The blazing water below them was pricked with midges.

'I don't want you to be alone,' Peter said.

'I shall be all right. I promise.'

'I thought you might like to come into the office. Not immediately, obviously, but – '

'No,' Kate said.

'Oh, I entirely understand. It was only a thought. The thing is, Kate, I want you to know that this isn't just a conventional thing. It may be expressed conventionally, but it's not a conventional thing. I don't claim to be the world's brightest.'

'You're fine,' Kate said. 'And thank you.'

'And I don't want thanks. Richard was my friend. You're his wife. I'll do anything I can to help you. I also happen to like you as a person.'

'As a person,' Kate said, 'do you?' She leaned and kissed him, across the distance that separated them. 'Thank you.'

She started them again on the walk to his house. It was about a quarter of a mile from hers; it too had a gate on to the towpath.

Peter said, 'Come in.'

Kate said, 'I must get back really. I would just like to thank Margaret again though, for all she did.'

Peter said, 'Yes, of course, the thing is, though, I don't think she'll be here.'

'Oh,' Kate said.

'I thought you knew?'

'I didn't,' Kate said, 'but I think I do now.'

'It's the culmination of something that's been coming for quite a while. That's why we haven't seen much of you lately, as a couple. I did indicate to Dick, but – '

'He may have – '

'He probably didn't want to upset you. I'm surprised in a way you didn't realize. It's a perfectly amicable arrangement. We just decided that all in all it would be better if we gave it a go separately. So Mag's living elsewhere for a bit. She comes home all the time to see Val and the bullfrog. Bullfrog! He'll be going to school next year. We shall have to find him a name soon!'

'Well damn you,' Kate said.

11

'Are you sure you wouldn't like me to stay?'

'Quite sure,' Kate said. 'Bill, have you got the food?'

'I'm not going to take it,' Bill said. 'I've thought about it.'

Mrs Sells said, 'You're sure you'll be all right?'

'I shouldn't think so,' Kate said, 'would you?'

Mrs Sells said, 'Has he given you something to take?'

'Not enough,' Kate said.

'I think I should come back,' Mrs Sells said.

'What are you trying to make me do?' Kate said. 'I remember you. You went home. We let you.'

'Yes,' her mother said. 'So you did. Come on, Bertie, in you get then, you great big man you.'

Bill said, 'I shall be home for half term or I'll come up at the weekend and see you, if you want?'

'Just be careful,' Kate said. 'Be careful, Mummy, won't you?'

'Don't worry about us,' her mother said. 'We shall be fine. Bill knows the way, don't you, Bill?'

Kate could see Richard in the lit windows. She walked up the shadows towards him.

'I seem to be the last,' Mr Morris said.

'Yes,' she said.

'I hoped I would be. I hung on. I hope you don't mind. I didn't like the idea of your being left. Don't worry, I'm not going to impose on you, but I want you to be free to be alone or otherwise. I wasn't having you left simply by accident, without anyone realizing.'

'That's nice of you,' Kate said. 'I'm glad you stayed.'

'I don't flatter myself, but strangers are sometimes a good idea.'

'You're not a stranger.'

'Oh yes,' he said. 'Allow me to introduce myself. I'm Bryan Morris.'

'I knew your son,' she said, pulling the trigger of her tears.

He held her. In the soft focus of her tears she could

believe him to be what she had lost, if only falsely and for a moment. She clung to a facsimile who made her young and old all at once. He was a stranger, this unsupple but still manly man, but he was not strange enough. He had the familiarity to disappoint, as well as to comfort.

'I'm going to stay here, if you'll have me, at least for tonight.'

She wanted him to go. 'All right,' she said. 'But you may be sorry.'

'You don't have to apologize,' he said. 'I understand. There's no call to be polite.'

'I shan't be that.'

'Even to be unwanted is still to serve some sort of function.' He was an educated man, but in the British way. It required a crisis for him to be driven to imagination. 'I had men killed around me in the war, you know,' Bryan Morris said. 'Friends. People I suppose you would say I didn't really know at all. Men of all sorts.'

'I suppose you must have,' Kate said. 'Unfortunately this is peace. In peace-time nothing seems more than an accident. Even love. Nothing has any sense.'

'Nor does it in war, believe me. Men still die – I'm sorry – they still die from pinpricks and survive the unbelievable. It none of it makes much sense. Why does one never talk about anything?'

'Wisdom,' Kate said.

'Fear,' said the old man. 'Fear, I fear. In my case, anyway. Fear of being tedious, of having been marked. Losing the herd. We're afraid of losing the herd. No longer running with the young bucks. Or whatever.'

'In my case,' Kate said. 'You're so horribly like him.'

42

'A parody,' Bryan Morris said, 'I know. Doesn't seem fair, does it? You could have done without me, really, I daresay, couldn't you?'

'And you me,' Kate said. 'Shall we drink something? You know what I want. Port. It's the only thing I could stomach. Any port in a storm. Why do we always repeat jokes we don't like?'

He said, 'My dear, you're very beautiful. I never saw it before. I saw that you were pretty, but I never saw that you were beautiful. You mustn't let anything change that.'

'It doesn't matter any more.' She recognized that she was prompting him. 'Not now.'

'After the war, after some of the things I had seen, I thought nothing much mattered. Petty things, petty problems, they didn't interest me much. We went for a holiday, my wife and I. She wasn't well even then and my return hadn't been all that easy. I don't have to elaborate. We went down to Devon. North Devon. What I'm going to tell you isn't the least remarkable. I went for a walk one afternoon, she was resting. And I found a seagull down on the shoreline. One of those long Devon beaches. It was covered with oil. As I say, it's a commonplace today. I took it back and started to clean it with some substitute turpentine and cotton wool. While I was doing it, my wife came down, poor Lilian, she came down from her rest and she took one look at me and do you know what she said?'

'What did she say?'

'She said, "Look at your jumper." I shall never forget it. "Look at your jumper." She was quite right, of course. It was black. "Look at your jumper." I shall never forget how she said it, Lil.'

43

'And what did you say?'

'Nothing. I said nothing.'

'And what did you think?'

'What did I think? It's a long time ago now. My God, I was in my forties. Do you know what I think I thought? I believe I thought: I'm old. It was rather a relief. I'm old, I thought; I shan't worry about ever wanting her again. I shall never want her again. You see, that had been part of our problem. Not uncommon. I thought, very well, my dear, that's that. No rancour, but that was that.'

'You never slept with her again?'

'Oh I wouldn't say that. Of course she became an invalid. I've always taken care of her. She never reproached me. I daresay there may have been the odd occasion when we, you know, did, but . . . '

'And you never – wanted anyone?'

'I remember finding you very attractive,' he said. 'You probably weren't aware. We had a talk one afternoon at your mother's place.'

'Stiles.'

'Yes, in the country. I thought, why should Richard have her? I wonder if you had any idea.'

'No,' Kate said, 'none. None.'

'Anyway, I was talking about marriage,' he said. 'The point being that I realized at that particular moment, that afternoon with the gull, that scars don't heal. They can't. Which wasn't at all, incidentally, the point I set out to make.'

'Which was?'

'Which was that trying to save that blasted gull made no real sense. I'd walked past men who were suffering ten times worse and called it duty or whatever. Hardened my heart. I can be very hard. It's what we were talking about. What struck me particularly was, there was absolutely no sense in what I did. No necessity. Nature is impersonal. Read it for meanings and it's absurd, callous, cruel, vindictive even. Certainly. And the lesson of that is, don't read it. Sitting with that dog of your mother's this afternoon –'

'Bertie?'

'Sitting with Bertie. She was petting it, calling it by its name, making a fuss of it ... I hope you don't mind me saying this?'

'Far from it.'

'People can mind,' he said. 'She went out, she went upstairs and there I was with this animal. I was thinking of nothing at all. I was sitting and it was sitting and I looked at it and I thought, you haven't got a name and I haven't got a name. You with your collar and I with my suit and we're both of us nameless. I didn't sleep much last night.'

'I know exactly what you mean,' Kate said. 'Bryan, if you want to go to bed, I shall be all right. All I dread is the phone.'

'I agree. It has the wrong note. You'd think they'd do something. No, I didn't mean I wanted to go up. I meant the way I seemed to be leaping about rather inconsequentially.'

'What happened to the gull?'

'The gull. Oh the gull! The gull died. The gull died. Yes.'

She gave the old man Bill's room. The spare room was cold. She put him to bed under Bill's Chelsea posters. She went into her bedroom, but she did not begin to undress. She waited until the old man had

45

finished in the bathroom and she had heard the click of his door. Her handbag was on the dressing-table. She pulled the curtains and then she opened the bag and drew from it a bunch of Freesia.

The stems were bound with silver paper; there was a poultice of cotton wool at their base. She took a card out of the bag too. On it was written: 'Love'. She stared at the card as if the text were very long or very complicated. She turned it over and read the blank side too. The flowers were compressed by their afternoon in the bag.

On the dressing-table were a tortoiseshell brush, comb and hand mirror; there was also a pair of Venetian bottles, red-bellied, crystal-stoppered. Kate laid the flowers on the mirror and opened the drawer and took out a pair of nail scissors. She held the flowers in her left hand and the scissors in her right. She sat on the stool (a Victorian stool with a buttoned top her mother had admired) and bent over the waste-basket with its scent of used tissues. Starting at the tip of the bunch, she cut the flowers into slivers, as if in obedience to an exacting recipe, and allowed them to fall into the silent basket. From time to time she looked at herself, without much interest, in the triple mirror.

12

'I think she must've lent Richard some books,' Kate said.

'Oh, I wasn't aware,' Peter Workman said. 'However, Miss Beale will almost certainly have sent on her

National Insurance card, assuming she had one, of course. I'll go and have a hunt.'

She had meant to come before. It was the only destination she had set herself, but she had not been able to get out of the house. She had no wish to stay in it, but she could not get out. She delayed dressing in the morning. She could not decide what to put on. At meal times, she would stand for minutes before a fridge containing only eggs and butter and milk and bacon and some marble cheese. She spent all day being patient with herself like her own lady companion.

Her father-in-law had gone the day after the funeral. In the morning he was old. His age was audible in the house. His deliberate breathing, his controlled cough, the way he clicked his fingernails as he 'tried to remember', these things reminded her of the wrong shade of a familiar colour. She was ready for loneliness.

She had no precise sense of what she had lost. Tears came and went; she had no warning of them. She no longer knew herself. She would put down a book and think, Good heavens, I've been reading. Sometimes she said it aloud, 'Good heavens, I've been reading,' and thought of a cuckoo, meaninglessly articulate.

The book lay on the hallstand. Several times she stood there, when Mrs Jenkins was hoovering, and watched herself in the thin mirror, her hand flat on the book. She might have been taking an oath. In the evenings, she took the book into the drawing-room and read it over and over. It was a curious duty. She did not go to find the girl's address until she knew the book well. It was her syllabus. When she had mastered it, she was ready to proceed.

'I think this must be it,' Peter said. 'This looks like it. Messrs Warde and Hancock. She didn't take too long to get fixed up.'

'Only Richard hated people who didn't return books.'

'I'll have it parcelled up for you and we'll bash it off to her.'

'Oh no,' she said.

She dressed quickly and neatly for her excursion. She wore her green linen suit and her long mackintosh. She drove fast, as she had before Richard's death. She parked the Vitesse some distance from the suburban address Peter had given her, in a street respectable with doctors. Warde and Hancock were in an old building. Only their window had been modernized by prosperity. A black screen displayed properties. The interior of the office could not be seen from the street. Kate looked at her watch: ten past five. She was armed with *Underground with the Oriole*. It was in her bag. She sat on a wall in front of a disused church. At twenty-five past, she crossed the street. There was a broad parade in front of the shops of which Warde and Hancock was one. A newsagent had placards out. One of the shops sold antiques: models of famous engines stood among ingenious Victorian shaving sets and dated Delft. The girl came out of the office. Kate was considering a vase. She allowed the girl to get some distance away. Then she followed. Beyond the shops, there was a new and narrower pavement. A supermarket, with a patio entrance, made a severe front on the road. The girl was standing in the patio. She was wearing a blue pinafore dress over a turtle-necked yellow jumper. Her lips moved as she remembered the things she wanted. Then she turned and went into the supermarket.

Kate took a basket. The lighting was very bright and white. It was so disagreeable that it must have been deliberate. Perhaps people bought more in a glare of unreality. Kate took things from the racks. She took a tin of pineapple and then she put it back. Richard liked pineapple; she did not. She took what she needed and bitterness played about her lips. She tested it on her face, like a cosmetic. She followed the girl. Music and advertisements cut in on each other. There was a smell of hot disinfectant. The girl shopped without hesitation, or interest.

Kate stood behind her in the queue. The girl's fingers curled the hair behind her ear. She did not smile at the cashier. She used no charm. As she emptied her basket, Kate slipped *Underground with the Oriole* into it.

'Yours, I think.'

The girl said, 'No, I – Oh!'

'Eighty-seven,' the cashier said.

Kate said, 'I think you lent it to my husband.'

The girl said, 'I'm sorry.'

'Richard,' Kate said.

The girl said, 'Excuse me.'

She paid and waited for the change. She waited for Kate too, while she paid. Kate was polite. She thanked the cashier.

'I'm Kate Morris.'

'Of course. I recognize you now. It was a bit of a surprise. Forgive me.'

'I would have seen you sooner, but you left.'

'Oh, the job. Yes, I left. I decided it was better.'

49

'Better?'

'I was going to write to you. I wanted to, but I decided perhaps I should not.'

'It was better,' Kate said.

'It was horrible what happened. Horrible.'

'Richard?'

'Horrible,' the girl said. 'I can't get over it.'

'I don't suppose it'll take long,' Kate said.

'You're wrong,' the girl said. 'You're wrong.'

'Ah!'

'I would like to go out of this place.'

Kate followed her into the patio. Drums of concrete were gaudy with geraniums. An old man sat on a bench, his chin crutched on an ash cane.

'In what way am I wrong?'

The girl searched Kate's face. And Kate worked to be bland. She stood stiff, as if a stranger were about to take something out of her eye.

'I think you know,' the girl said.

'I assure you you're wrong,' Kate said. Her eyes were on the book the girl was holding. The girl looked down at it. 'Will you please come with me? I should like to talk to you.'

'No. There is no point.'

'You misunderstand. I want you to come with me.'

'I understand,' the girl said. 'And there is no point.'

'My car is round the corner. I want you to come. Now.'

'I cannot, I am sorry.'

'I insist,' Kate said.

'Insist?' It was a new word to the girl. It surprised her; she tucked it under her chin like a violin.

'I think I have a right,' Kate said.

'I don't think so.'

'To talk to you? I think I do. But somewhere other than in the street. Perhaps we can find a cup of tea.'

'Oh, if you like,' the girl said.

13

'Anything to eat?'

'Anything to eat? This seems rather a nice place. Oh look, they've got those dipped chocolate things . . . '

'Please, you have something. Do you have sandwiches?'

'Ham, cheese, tomato, egg.'

'Egg.'

'And for you?'

'Nothing for me,' Kate said. 'Just tea.'

'Oh, I . . . ' the girl said.

'And one egg sandwich. What made you choose to come and work round here?'

'I live quite close.'

'You had quite a journey then. To – to where you were working before.'

'Twenty-five minutes.'

'On your bicycle.'

'Usually. Unfortunately it is not a very good bicycle.'

'You were with him, weren't you? When it happened.'

'Yes.'

'I mean, there's no sense in pretending . . . '

'I do not pretend.'

'No. Ah, here's the tea. Doesn't that look good? That does look good. You went up with him.'

'Yes. I often went with him.'

'Quite. Milk?'

'Oh yes, this time I take a little milk.' She tossed her head. 'No sugar.'

'Do you get fat?'

'No. Because I don't take sugar.' The girl smiled, a soft blow at Kate's severity.

'I want you to explain something to me, Miss Clavand.'

'Miss Clavand!'

'Am I to call you something else?'

'Not at all!'

'I want you to explain something to me, because I'm anxious to understand.'

'If I can.'

'It's this: how – how could you just go and leave him?'

The girl seemed to be stirring the question into her tea. She then tasted this little recipe that Kate had devised.

'Now I will ask you something,' she said.

'Don't you think you owe me an answer?'

She made the same face as she had at Kate's insistence. 'My question is a sort of answer. Of all the things that I could have done, do you think that leaving him was the easiest for me to do? Are you wise, Madame, to have chosen to believe just that?'

Kate said, 'Explain to me what I should have believed.'

'You know the answer to that better than I do. You can express it better than I can.'

'I think you misunderstand my reasons for – for finding you. All I want to know is what happened.'

'You know what happened,' the girl said. 'He had a heart attack.'

'A heart attack, yes, we've established that. But I should like to know the exact circumstances.'

'He had a heart attack. He was in very much pain. They sent for the ambulance. There, now!'

'I don't mean to upset you,' Kate said, 'but who exactly sent for the ambulance? You? Or the hotel?'

'I phoned down, they called the ambulance; I ask them to get a doctor, they said an ambulance would be better; they sent for the ambulance.'

'And you?'

'Waited with him.'

'With Richard. And how did he seem then? Here, borrow one of mine.'

'He was in pain. I'm all right. I'm O.K. He was lying down. I tell him help is coming. What does it matter?'

'It matters to me,' Kate said, 'quite considerably. One day you may understand. I hope you never do.'

'I understand, of course. But what is the point?'

'My husband is dead,' Kate said. 'How do you think it feels to think that if, if people had behaved differently he might still be alive today?'

'I have deceived you,' the girl said.

'That's hardly the point, is it?'

'Sorry, not deceived. Disappointed. Because I did not run away and leave him to be discovered by somebody else. Is that what you were hoping?'

'I was hoping nothing.'

'I am not what you think,' the girl said. 'What you

53

want to think.' She pressed loose white and yolk together with braced fingers. 'You see?' She threw her head up and searched Kate's face again. 'So that's the end of that.'

Kate said, 'Are you sure you won't have something else?'

'Oh . . . ' She was embarrassed for Kate. She had money in a purse with a drawstring.

'That'll be all right,' Kate said, but the girl threw two loud coins on the plate and was out of the door. Kate picked the coins from beside the red crusts on the girl's plate. Hanging beside the door was a gauze sleeve for a charity. She put the coins in that.

14

That evening Kate sat at the kitchen table with her face against the Formica and longed for pain. She bent and stretched her body in the void for some stab of relief. She walked round the garden under the singing sky and cut the dead heads. She wanted to fall, to feel bruises. The calm wracked her. She was sick with it. She wanted no company. She wanted no comfort. She wanted pain.

She showed herself their slides. She tested her heart against every blade she possessed. She had given Richard a two-sided slide-box for his last birthday. He was good with a camera. There were more pictures of her, and of Bill, than of him. She was always centred, or nicely caught against a foreign building. She herself took photographs in a hurry. Richard's face wore a look of hooked apprehension; her sudden click had jerked up his head and there he was, gaping. The projector had a button to adjust the focus. The adjustment seemed to bring him narrowly to life and then he was blurred again. She left him on the icy screen and went up to it. She steeped herself in the light. He lay on her and pinned her in a weightless vice. She put in no new slides. She left the last of him on the screen and crouched and stared at him until she ached. She crouched in a tight, torturer's box. 'We were happy,' she said. 'We were happy. We were. We were. We were.'

15

The girl left the office as usual. It was a fine evening. She walked to the bus stop, her tote-bag dangling an inch above the dry pavement, and then she walked on, shrugging. After a few streets, the road veered towards the river. A cobbled slipway went down to where barges loaded. An eight came boring through the centre arch of the bridge. The girl did not look at the oarsmen. She walked on beside the granite wall, swinging from time to time for the bus that would be no help to her now.

She lived in a side-road lined with mutilated trees. The houses were at the bottom of narrow, deep gardens. There were children's slides and swings in most of them. The houses were Victorian, but they had been renovated with bright doors and composition windowboxes. The gate of the double-fronted house where the girl lived was canary yellow.

The next day, it was drizzling. She stayed later than usual at work. Perhaps she hoped it would stop. When she came out, she was wearing a yellow P.V.C. windcheater and a coal-scuttle hat to match. She huddled and went with little steps towards the bus stop, to avoid wetting her knees. She sheltered in the doorway of a laundry, until the bus came shearing through the wet.

The brick of the house was sullen with the rain.

Kate said, 'Miss Clavand. Miss Clavand.'

Kate was sitting in the Vitesse. The windows were misted. She had outdistanced the bus. The car looked empty. There was no one else in the street. Kate opened the door of the car as the girl came level. She bent down, but did not get in.

'Not another book?'

Kate said, 'Please get in. I want to apologize.'

'There is no need. I understand.'

'This is where you live, is it?'

'Yes,' the girl said. 'You want to come in? During the day it's quite quiet.'

'No, I won't do that.' The girl bent down with a smile to shut the door and saw Kate. 'Did I do something?'

'No. Nothing.'

'You followed me here,' the girl said. 'You followed me here.'

'I told you. I wanted to apologize.'

'No, you didn't,' the girl said. 'Of course you didn't. That's not at all what you wanted.' She sat down on the rain-spattered seat, knees half out of the car. 'I am not surprised,' she said. 'Now I am not surprised . . . '

'At what?'

'He was so afraid. He was in pain. I have never seen a man in pain like that and he was so afraid. Afraid of you, I mean. Afraid you would find out. He begged me to go. I will never forget it.'

'So you went.'

The girl was ugly with disgust. Tears ran along the gutter of her eyelids. 'Once he was in the hospital I saw there was nothing else to do. I had them call you and then I went away. He wanted me to go. I went. What should I do?'

'How did you get back to London?'

'I hitch-hiked,' the girl said. 'I hitch-hiked.'

'But you drove the car to the hospital, I take it?'

'Yes. You know, it seems unbelievable, but I had an idea, an idea, that they would do something and he would be all right. I thought perhaps it was a cramp or a crisis of the liver. And I would be able to take him home, back to the hotel. Of course, once I was at the hospital, and I was told . . . '

'You didn't think to take the car back.'

'I couldn't drive.'

'You drove it there.'

'Yes,' the girl said. 'You must have known something was going on.'

'Wives generally do.'

'Yes.' The girl pulled her knees in out of the rain. 'I don't suppose it was exactly the first time, was it?'

57

16

Kate started the car. The rain watered the windscreen. The windows were misted. She reached across the girl and locked her door.

The girl said, 'What are you doing now? Where are we going?'

Kate twisted the knob for the wipers. She cuffed at the fogged windows with an old duster, part of a car-cleaning pack Bill had given her. She offered the girl a promising smile. She drove fast once more. As they went, she drew the safety belt across the girl and threw the short end into her lap.

She drove home.

'This is my house,' she said. 'This is my house. This is where we lived. This was our place. This one, here. Right here. This is where we lived. For fourteen years. Richard and I.'

They sat by the kerb outside the house. Kate made no move to get out of the car.

'We loved each other,' Kate said. 'Don't you dare try to destroy that. We were together for twenty years. Do you really think you counted for much against twenty years of life?'

The girl said, 'I never thought so.'

'You didn't know us,' Kate said. 'You don't know anything about us. We had something neither of us could ever have had without the other.'

'I never pretended,' the girl said. She sat with her

knees drawn up to her chin. She chewed at her knuckles. Kate masked her tears – anger, anger – with a driver's anxiety. She backed the car closer to the pavement.

The girl said, 'He wanted to tell you. He wanted to tell you everything always.'

'I'm going to take you home now,' Kate said.

'He hated lies. It hurt him to tell lies. He was always saying so.'

'It didn't worry you, I dare say.'

'I don't tell lies. I have nothing I have to tell anyone. No one I have to tell. When did I tell lies?'

'Never mind,' Kate said.

'He was never going to leave you or anything like that.'

'Is something the matter with you? You seem very . . . Are you suffering from some sort of . . . ?'

'I am a bit frightened in cars, that's all. My father was injured once. I was with him.'

'Badly?'

'No, but . . . I saw blood. On his face and his hands. Especially his hands.'

'I shan't hurt you,' Kate said.

'Why do you hate me?' the girl said.

'Do I?'

'Oh please. Of course.'

'Oh please, isn't it rather obvious?'

'I did everything I could. No one could have done anything. I loved him.'

'I loved him,' Kate said. 'So there we are.'

They had to stop at the lights. As they waited, someone rapped on Kate's window. She rolled down the window.

'When the lights change, go across the crossing and then pull over to the side.'

They sat.

'I never saw him, did you?' Kate said.

The girl shrugged. Her face was clouded. She looked as ugly as she knew how.

The policeman said, 'What speed were you doing up past the Robin Hood Gate, any idea?'

Kate said, 'I'm sorry. I was just keeping up, I thought.'

'That's what everyone thinks. You were doing over fifty miles an hour. Fifty-three to be precise. Do you know what the limit is on that particular stretch?'

'I believe it's forty,' Kate said.

'And I believe you're right. Forty miles an hour.'

'I'm sorry,' Kate said.

'Sorry I stopped you,' the policeman said, 'or sorry you were going too fast?'

'I suppose you're right.'

'It's not the first time I've seen you on this particular stretch of road, is it?'

'I can't say,' Kate said. 'I can't say that I remember you.'

'Your number will be made a note of,' the policeman said. 'But I shan't report you on this occasion. Kindly be more careful next time.'

'Yes,' Kate said. 'Thank you. I'm sorry. I will be.'

'And will you?' the girl said, once they were moving again.

'No,' Kate said. 'I'm sorry to say probably not.'

The girl said, 'Do you like funny stories?'

'It depends if they're funny.'

'This one is quite funny, I think. It's a true story. About a friend of my father who works in London,

60

Claude Thiviers. He is some kind of an international lawyer, I think. Anyway, one day he is driving very fast down Park Lane in his Jaguar and a policeman stops him, like just now. The cop comes up to him and asks him the same question. "How fast do you think you were going, etcetera?" But very angry. Claude looks very apologetic, very foreign and he starts to mutter about how sorry he is – and was he really going too fast – and all this business, but in a very thick French accent, almost incomprehensible really, until eventually the policeman says to him, "You're not English, sir, are you?" '

'Very funny,' Kate said.

'No, the funny part is coming now. Claude says, no as a matter of fact. Then the policeman explains to him very slow and very clearly. "Well, sir," he says, "in – this – country – in built-up areas – in the towns and the cities – we drive at – thirty, that's 3, o – miles an hour. We do *not* – drive – quickly. We – drive – slowly. Do you understand, sir?" "Yes, yes," Claude says, "I'm sorry, from now on I remember." "Very well, sir," says the policeman, "enjoy your stay in England." "Zank you, very much," Claude says, and he is about to drive away when the policeman realizes that he is all the time driving an English car with an English licence, and he taps on the window and Claude rolls it down again and the policeman says, "Excuse me, sir, but – how – long – have – you – been – in – this – country?" Claude looks him straight in the eye and says, "As a matter of fact, about thirty-two years." '

'That *is* funny,' Kate said.

'Isn't it?' the girl said. 'Isn't it? Of course if you

61

know Claude, it's better. He is such a funny man. He is funny and funny things happen to him. But really such a nerve! Thirty-two years. Imagine his face! It's funny, isn't it?' She was biting her knuckles again and shaking her head and she looked very young and very charming, as if she herself had not been in England for more than a day.

17

'I'm sorry to say I've never in my life been so deliriously happy.'

'You certainly look as though you are,' Kate said.

'Kate, I'm so happy, I really wish – I really don't know what to do.' Margaret Workman spread her hands and clapped them together as if to start a race. 'That's the honest truth.'

'Then what're you sorry about?'

'Oh, I suppose sitting in your garden, consuming your vittles and talking about happiness when you're – well, naturally in the state you are.'

'That's my problem.'

'Not just yours. I was supposed to come here and cheer you up, but I have a terrible feeling it must sound like gloating. I suppose, quite honestly, it's horribly true. I am gloating. I'm so happy to be happy. It's a sort of double thing.'

'You certainly look ten years younger.'

'Oh God, is that all? I put in for at least fifteen.

Nemmind. It's a start. You must have had some ink-ling, didn't you, that this was brewing?'

'Of course,' Kate said, 'one isn't blind.'

'We tried terribly hard, poor Peter and I, to be like you and Richard, but we were never really within miles.'

'How long have you been married?'

'Oh time, what does time matter? Heavens, it must be fifteen years. Fifteen years. Long enough to know. Long enough to know better quite frankly. I can imagine how you feel.'

'Would you like some more ham and stuff?'

'Oh no, that was tons. I'm not a big eater midday. We generally have our main nosh at night, when the day's tantrums are done. Life at the Centre, my dear, is one round of dramas, it's amazing. The energy creative people can put into cutting each other's throats. David's fantastically tactful, but that only means everyone's always coming and dumping their little probbos on his plate. You must meet him.'

'How are you managing with the children?'

'Fantastically well as it turns out. We've got a tremendous girl, which helps.'

'It must.'

'Helga. She's tremendous.'

'But the children themselves?' Kate said.

'Have been amazingly sensible about the whole thing. We've discussed it quite frankly with them. They know exactly what's going on. Peter and I both agree that the most damaging thing is doubt. As long as people know where they are, they can cope. What creates half the trouble in the world is people being uncertain.'

63

Kate said, 'How old is the Bullfrog now?'

'The Bullfrog's nearly five. He'll be five in August.'

'And you explained to him – ?'

'Not everything. Not all the ins and outs. We explained that Mummy was going to work full time and she wouldn't always be at home to give him breakfast, but that she still loved him very very much. He knows where he stands, that's the real thing.'

'And Valerie?'

'Val the same,' Margaret said. 'Except that I explained a little further, not much further, because I think that can be an indulgence. I also discussed it all with David. He said he thought it could be an indulgence to tell people too much, a sort of unconscious vanity, he said, which I think is a very intelligent point and not one that people often make. He can be terribly sane.'

'I take it he's married too.'

'At our age everyone's married,' Margaret said. 'In spite of the health warning on the packet. You don't mind me being honest, do you? Only we've been friends for so long.'

'We may as well start sometime,' Kate said.

'This is nice wine. Nice and fruity. I don't like it too rarefied. I'm a girl with coarse tastes, I'm afraid. What do you mean, start sometime? I think we've always been reasonably honest actually, in so far as married people can be.'

'Does marriage make it difficult to be honest?'

'Across frontiers I think it does,' Margaret said. 'And within them very often. Everyone's always working so hard to give off plus vibrations. One hides the cracks like a man selling second-hand china. One's never a separate person in a marriage, really, is one? Tactless Mag, there I go! Only that's part of friendship too, isn't it, knowing when to be tactless? If you and I can't talk about what's happened – acknowledge what's happened, as David always calls it – then who can?'

Kate said, 'I suppose you're right.'

'You and I can afford not to have secrets. It's not as though you worked at the Beeb. The circular gossip factory, David calls it. Among other things! Isn't it funny how you fall into these abbreviations? When I first heard that particular monstrosity, the Beeb, I thought, ugh! never under any circumstances! And here I am beebing away. No willpower whatever. Thank God in view of certain things that've happened, but still! You ought to take a job, you know that, don't you?'

'What can I do?'

'I knew you'd say that. A capable person like you. What man would ever say a thing like that? You've been brainwashed. There are lots of things you can do. A woman with a degree . . .'

'My degree is worth precisely nothing,' Kate said. 'It's as much use as my medal for coming second in the South London Inter-Schools hundred yards.'

'I never knew you did that. Quick off the mark, were you? Of course you could get work if you wanted to. Peter always says how efficient you are. All I mean is, you must make a life for yourself. You mustn't think of doing nothing as being a sort of loyalty to Richard.'

'I think I'll go and make some coffee,' Kate said. 'You'll have some coffee, won't you?'

Margaret followed her down the steps into the kitchen. The two halves of the coffee machine were tight. Kate made it a labour to separate them.

Margaret said, 'Can I help?'

'One person has to do it,' Kate said. 'Richard always screwed it together so hard, he was the only person who could undo it.' The boat was still in the garden, one side unpainted. Margaret put her hand to Kate's shoulder, but Kate was not to be touched. 'That's got it!'

Margaret said, 'Kate, I really want your advice.'

'Advice is never a problem,' Kate said. 'Provided you promise not to take it.'

'I can think of so many men who would give anything for a woman as amusing as you can sometimes be.'

'Advice about what exactly?'

'I suppose what it boils down to is this: can anyone really make a success of a marriage with someone a good deal younger than themselves?'

'How old is he, the particular man?'

'David's twenty-eight.'

Kate said, 'And the woman? Some people can't make a success of any kind of marriage. Others . . . '

'You think I'm a bitch,' Margaret said, 'don't you? Be honest!'

'On the contrary.'

'Leaving Peter. And now thinking about marrying David. Well, let me tell you I have very few illusions, very few illusions indeed. The illusions are all on the other side, as it happens. Personally, I'd be quite happy to go on as we are. To tell you the truth, it gives me everything I want. The pressure happens to be all the other way. David's marriage is a total mess;

66

it has been from the start, and he feels it very keenly. Any failure hurts him dreadfully. When something's beyond repair, his instinct is to junk it. He can actually be quite ruthless. I've seen him with a producer or a director, he's patience itself up to a certain point and then, when the thing's beyond saving, wham! axe time! That's the point he's reached with Deirdre.'

'Deirdre!'

'I'm afraid so. They haven't lived together properly for three years. She's down in the country; he's in Cranley Gardens: it's the full disaster!'

'Do they have children?'

'Three.'

'From the start! He was a bit slow, wasn't he, turning off the juice?'

'She insisted. Turning off the juice! I've never heard that one before. The thing was, she wanted three children before she was twenty-seven and then finish, that was the idea. She used to be an actress; she figured that way she could go back eventually. Anyway, never mind who's to blame, he's sick of being pulled three ways. The way things are going for him, he needs to be able to give all his energy to the job. If he can only do that, the sky's the limit. Or at least the sixth floor, which is as near the sky as anyone can get, apart from the man who sweeps the roof.'

Kate said, 'If you want to marry him, marry him. In the end, isn't that about all there is to be said? And if you don't, don't. Especially the latter.'

'Listen, personally, I'm happy to go on as we are. It suits me much the best, quite frankly, because there's no conflict of loyalties.'

'Do you want cream in this?'

'I shouldn't. Just a drop. Little more. Perfect. In the sense that if you marry somebody, it's different. I don't know why it should be, but we all know it is. Unavoidable. This way, I can regulate how I dispose of my time and there's no one to say I'm wrong. I don't feel I'm letting anybody down. Also, my experience is, as soon as people are tied down, they want to break out. Even if they're responsible for tying the knot. Don't you agree?'

Kate said, 'I liked being married.'

'You had Richard,' Margaret said.

'So I'm not a good judge,' Kate said.

'Well, believe me, it's true. Lovely coffee. Were you honestly never remotely tempted in all the years?'

'Tempted?'

'Tempted. To leave the rails. Never? I must say you always looked like the cat that had the cream. I've never known anyone who could be silent so eloquently. I used to envy you like mad. You wouldn't say more than a few words all evening and men would come up to me afterwards and say, "Isn't she fascinating?" and there was I beating my brains out to be witty and captivating and you were the one they fancied.'

'When?' Kate said. 'Who? I wasn't aware.'

'Simon Urquhart.'

'Simon Urquhart?'

'You remember Simon Urquhart, with the beard, at that shindig we gave, God, two years ago now it must be. The schoolmaster who'd been on the box a couple of times.'

'He was dreadful, if it's the one I think he was. He smoked a pipe and talked about radical rethinks.'

'He's never forgotten you. Quite an interesting man actually. David's used him a couple of times for one or two things. And of course, there's Peter.'

'What?'

'Who's always been smitten with you.'

'He's always been nice to me. Because I was Richard's wife.'

'You don't seriously think he's as nice to everybody as he is to you, do you? Because I can promise you he isn't. Of course, he knows you like him. There isn't anything he wouldn't do for you. Goodness me, is that really the time? That's what actors always say; old joke in the profession. You know, big takum! But seriously, I must be on the wing. We've got a dreaded conference with the new supersuper. He's put in for a job in Scotland and my dear the amount of good luck we've been wishing him! Three years under the kilt's just what he needs. Kate, promise me something.'

'Well?'

'That if ever you need me, you'll call. Never mind if I can be a bore. Bores can sometimes help you realize how lucky you are; even if it's only when they leave. Goodbye, darling. Quite apart from that, you must meet Peter sometime.'

'Peter?'

'David. Did I say Peter? I am a fool. He's so bright; I know you'll like him. You'd better!'

'You've got a new car,' Kate said.

'Oh, the Freedom Bus! Do you like it? Still waiting for its first scratch. Well, I must go or I shall miss the children. I always make a point of meeting them out of school and then it's back to the grind.'

'Give them my love,' Kate said.

69

'Dear Kate, don't disapprove too much.'

'I don't disapprove,' Kate said.

'Of course you do,' Margaret said. 'I expected you to.'

18

She broke a dish putting the lunch things in the machine. It slipped through her fingers, one of the white Denby-ware they had had ever since they were married. She watched it crash. She regretted it, and she wanted to follow it with the rest of them, bang on the tiles. She wanted no trace of that lunch, least of all the penance of clearing it. Margaret's happiness was an assault she could bear. What left her resentful was the dullness that the other woman's kindness enjoined upon her. The pleasure of David was not enough for her on its own. Margaret could have continued to enjoy him without anyone ever knowing, but only with half the enjoyment. Her lust for publicity did not offend Kate; she did not even condemn it, but she disliked being expected to condemn it. She despised a freedom that flourished only on comparisons and a love that depended on boasting, but she did not resent them. She resented only that Margaret thought that she and Kate were friends. She resented being congratulated on being sensible and confirmed in being ordinary. She resented that with bitter anger and a deadly sense of loss, a sense of loss and humiliation that she had not felt since Erica.

In her sleep she still went to the cot and found her. But in her sleep, and it happened that night, with punctual cruelty, she found her alive. She picked her up and carried her to the room where Richard was. Richard was alive too, and she handed the baby to him and made to join him in the narrow bed. He was in a single bed. He wore his old red pyjamas (he called them his boat club pyjamas, because his college colours were bright red) and he took the baby and turned from her with it, so that Erica was lost from her sight, and he was gone too, and he lay down, very flat, and she saw that the bed was made and there was no one in it. Both of them had gone.

She knew the solution. She was already awake when she woke, or so it seemed, and became the spectator of her own despair. She knew that she was awake as she flung herself sideways on to the empty space beside her, acting normal. She reminded herself of the empty room and clutched the headless pillow. There was nothing she could tell Margaret. How dare she pretend to understand! She would never tell Margaret anything.

19

'Well, how do we stand as of whenever?' Peter said. 'Are we in the red or in the black?'

'You know as well as I do,' Kate said. 'Things are quite rosy.'

'Rosy black, I hope! Kate, I'm damned grateful to you, you know that, don't you, for coming down? I realize it must have been a hell of a strain for you. You're good stuff.'

'Peter, I did want to talk to you about it.'

'Here I am. Talk. I'm all ears. The doctor says there's nothing he can do, so there we are. Call me Dumbo.'

Kate said, 'I'm sure the accountant could manage all the paperwork without having me as a sort of halfway house.'

'He can do it standing on his head, if the money's right, but that's not really the point.'

'I don't want a job manufactured for me,' Kate said. 'However well-intended.'

'It isn't like that at all,' Peter said. 'No one's doing that.'

'I want something only I can do,' Kate said. 'I never exactly did the books because they were a vocation. I did them because –'

'Because it helped Richard. God, I see that. I'm not a fool. I quite realize that. In other words, you want to stop.'

'I don't want to put you on the spot. I'm perfectly willing to carry on *pro tem*, if it helps.'

'But it's not exactly what you're looking for. I do appreciate that. It does help actually. And personally, of course, I'm a bit biased. It means at least I've got Wednesdays to look forward to. I gather you saw Margaret.'

'Yes. She came to lunch.'

'It's all working quite well. As I told you, it is all perfectly amicable, which is a blessing. No fireworks,

72

no recriminations. And a lot less friction. All very civilized.'

'I'm sure that's the best way,' Kate said.

'No question of it. Good God, nobody deliberately sets out to hurt anybody, do they? It's a combination of circumstances. Kate, listen, let's have dinner sometime and really chew the fat.'

'What a vile-sounding idea!'

'Have a proper talk, I mean. Sorry. If it wouldn't be a bore for you, it'd be a treat for me. Men dream of being bachelors again, but take it from me, there's not much gilt on that particular gingerbread, at least not when you've got a waistline like mine. How about tomorrow?'

'Tomorrow,' Kate said. 'Tomorrow . . .'

'Or Friday. If you're not free tomorrow.'

'I'm going to a sale with my mother, but I should be back. No, tomorrow's O.K.'

'I'll come by for you. I don't want to be a bore. I don't want to intrude or anything. If you'd rather leave it, we can leave it.'

'No, no,' Kate said. 'I'd like to. Don't feel that. Peter, what's happening about that client, the one Richard went to see?'

'Rupert Hollins. Yes, that's something else I've got to cope with in due course.'

'Because they phoned apparently. Your girl was telling me.'

'Right! That's something I've got to cope with. I'll call him in the morning. I did write and explain, of course, but ... Well, my problem. Have you got transport?'

'I've got my car. The Alvis is still in Ipswich.'

'Good God, I'll go and fetch it for you. No bother.'

'What, and have no one left in the office at all?'

'No bother. I can always combine it with going to see friend Hollins.'

'I'll go up and get it sometime. I don't exactly need it.'

'What a bugger,' Peter said. 'These machines, aren't they? Never where you want them. Well ... ' He put his arm round her as she put on her coat to go. 'Till tomorrow.' He kissed her cheek with an old-fashioned chuck of the lips. 'We'll forget our troubles. See if we can anyway.'

20

It was a narrow attic under the sharp roof. There was a long bedsitter and a cloakroom-cum-kitchen and a shared bathroom with an Ascot. In the main room was an old sofa and matching armchair, rust-coloured and prolapsed, and a modern divan under the end window which looked on to a cemetery. The ironing board was up. Books and records filled some footless, handmade shelves under the dormer window over the front garden.

'Please sit down.'

Kate said, 'I haven't really come to stay. Have you been here long?'

'Yes, quite a long time.'

'It's nice. It's a nice shape.'

'Provided you're triangular,' the girl said. 'It's too small really.'

'I'll tell you why I called.'

'You don't want to borrow a book?'

'No, I don't want to do that. It's about the job.'

'The job.'

'The job you were doing before. At, at Workman and Morris, with . . .'

'May I offer you at least some tea?'

'Are you going to make it?'

'Of course, this is my place. I put the kettle on.'

'I'm sure you enjoyed it more than the one you're doing now. I mean, quite apart from, from what was happening; as a job, I mean.'

'The present job is a nothing.'

'You must hate it.'

'No.'

'And that's why I thought I ought to come and see you. I didn't mean to intrude and I shan't stay long.'

'Oh boff!' The girl pouted. 'I have nothing to do. I was going to wash my hair.'

'I shan't stay long. I think they could really do with you if you wanted to go back, that's the point. I spoke to Peter Workman about it and he seems very ready.'

The girl said, 'Thank you. I could never go back. Quite impossible.'

'Only the man phoned from where you'd been, you and Richard, up in the country. He asked for you. And that made me think . . . What was it he called you? Something funny he knew you as!'

'Mijo?' the girl said.

'That must've been it. You obviously made an impression.'

'Oh boff!' She said it again. On her own ground, she was a schoolgirl: blue pinafore, open-necked white shirt, bare feet. 'A type like that . . .'

'That's short for Marie-José, is it?'

'It's quite common,' she said. 'It's nothing special.'

'I thought I owed it to you at least to tell you,' Kate said. 'Forgive me asking, but how did you make this tea?'

'It's not good? Oh my God, the tea! I forgot the tea.'

'It did seem a bit weak.'

'I forgot to put in the tea. I am so sorry. I never often have it. But generally at least I remember to put some tea in it.'

'It's relatively unimportant,' Kate said. 'Truly.'

'Have you had supper?' the girl said.

'I don't eat a lot at the moment,' Kate said.

'Me neither. I make something for both of us. Are you still angry?'

'Was I angry?'

'Yes, I think so,' the girl said. 'With me at least you don't have to pretend. If I make an omelette? I can make omelettes. I try and remember to put the eggs in.'

Kate said, 'I'd love an omelette.'

'Then I do it,' the girl said.

'I wonder why you stay in England.'

'To earn money, and to save it. One day I want to travel. You can't live on air.'

'Aren't there jobs you could do in France?'

'It's experience to work here,' the girl said. 'I learn English and . . . In France, I just work. Now I don't know what I shall do. At least for the moment though I don't have to explain myself to anyone or be nice to people.'

The girl brought the omelette in the pan. She had plates bracketed under one arm and knives and forks under her chin. Kate rescued the plates and the girl halved the omelette.

Kate said, 'It's good.'

'An omelette, what's an omelette?'

'Only I think that's about as much as I can do.'

'I did only three eggs for two people.'

'All the same, thank you. It was delicious, but . . . '

The girl blanked her own plate with a piece of sliced bread.

Kate said, 'How long had it been going on?'

'A little while. A month, two months . . . '

'Surely you know.'

'About two months.'

'He used to eat here with you sometimes, didn't he?'

'It happened,' the girl said. 'Not often. Once, twice, maybe three times.'

'Do you always approach the truth by degrees?'

'I'm sorry?'

'It never happened before,' Kate said. 'Never. Not in twenty years.'

'Ah!' the girl said. 'I understand.' Kate was staring at her. 'Some cheese?'

'I must go,' Kate said.

The girl grinned, but not at Kate. 'Stay, and talk,' she said. 'I don't mind. I have nothing –'

'*You* don't mind.'

'You can say anything you like to me,' the girl said. 'I make some coffee. I make coffee better than tea.'

Kate said, 'I promise you, I don't want anything. Nothing at all. I have no doubt that you do things very capably, but I truly don't want a thing.'

'He came here only when we had been working, on his way home. When he would be late anyway.'

'That's a comfort to know,' Kate said. 'Or are you being kind?'

'Truthful,' the girl said. 'Like him.'

'But he lied,' Kate said.

'I did not hear. The tap was running.'

'Nothing. Nothing.'

'He was afraid always that you would not understand. He wanted you to know everything.'

'Did he?' Kate said.

'Oh I think so,' the girl said.

'You're not a Parisian,' Kate said, 'are you?'

'Parisienne, no. Why do you ask? I come from the Périgord, a small town. Saint-Cyprien. I think you were there once.'

'We camped on the river.'

'That's right!'

Kate laughed, in spite of herself. 'You'd think you'd been there with us. We borrowed a friend's caravan and we went all over. I expect you know.'

'You were very happy on that holiday.'

'We were often very happy,' Kate said. 'I asked because suddenly you looked like a country girl. Very innocent. And very dangerous.'

'Dangerous? I don't think so. To what? Only because you think of what he and I were, you think of that as a danger to you. It was never that. A threat.'

'I don't know that I think of it at all.'

'You think of it a lot,' the girl said. 'And you are wrong.'

'I gave Richard twenty years. Twenty years. I gave him twenty years.'

'And you took twenty years. And you took twenty years. So?'

'I don't believe in your ideas,' Kate said. 'I'm not French about these things.'

'You despised him,' the girl said.

'I loved him,' Kate said.

'You despised him.'

'I'm going now, Miss Clavand. I'll help you wash the things up and then I'm going. I don't really think – '

'You want to despise me too. You want to believe that I am a nobody, a little French nothing. It is unthinkable to you that he could have cared for anyone worthwhile. Because you believe that he was not worthwhile either. Well?'

'I'm not going to argue with you.'

'You have no right to despise me, Madame.'

'Do you seriously think you meant anything to him? You – you were simply a girl. He was a man and you were simply a young girl . . .'

'And you were not,' the girl said.

21

'I must go,' Kate said.

'Are you all right?'

'Yes, I'm all right. I'm all right. Very unworthy. Very undignified. Very unEnglish. What must you think of me?'

'Oh poof, what does it matter?'

'I ought to be at home,' Kate said.

The girl went about clearing the room: cups, dishes, the pan. She came back from the little kitchen with a cigarette unlit between pouting lips and collected crumbs in a cupped hand.

Kate said, 'You're very neat. Tidy.'

'No, some days I can't do anything. Some days I can do nothing; I am nothing; a speck, you know?'

'That's what we are, isn't it, specks? Like flies to wanton boys. Do you read a lot of poetry?'

'Yes, I like it rather a lot.'

'I used to read a lot of poetry. Once. That book you lent Richard, is that a particular favourite of yours?'

'No, not particularly. It was lent to me as a matter of fact by someone who lives right here, in this house, an American. He saw it here and I said go ahead, take it, Josh won't mind, so he took it. I think he liked it rather a lot.'

'Sometimes I hate him,' Kate said.

'He loved you,' the girl said.

'As if he had walked out, as if it were something deliberate, as if he had deliberately gone missing. I think of him the day that he was going up to, to Ipswich; I think back to the morning he was leaving and I think "You said nothing. You said you'd be back and – "'

'He was coming back, madame.'

'Madame!' Kate said. 'I know, I know. I think of people in court, you know, in trials? They sometimes get asked, "Was he any different that morning?" and they always say, "He didn't seem at all different." And then he goes and never comes back, like a man walking out of a shop.'

'No one knows they are going to die,' the girl said. 'So what can they do?'

'Everyone knows they are going to die,' Kate said.

'So what can they do?'

'Have you ever tried to describe anybody, without looking at them, without a photograph, out of your own mind?'

'Not often.'

'That's another thing I try to do. I sit and I think if only I could describe him fully enough, I should be able to have him back again. When I was a little girl, once at school, there was a girl, a friend of mine, I thought, and she had something I knew was mine. It was actually a little model – I can see it now – of a horse and rider, a mass-produced thing, nothing very exceptional, but I was very fond of it – and I said to her, her name was Geraldine, I said to her, "That's mine," and she put it behind her back and she said, "No, it isn't." Geraldine Laver. She was a very pretty blonde girl, with a little doll's face, and a lovely singing voice, anyway – she said it was hers, and I said it wasn't and she said, "If it's yours, you must be able to describe it," and I said of course I could describe it and I said what it was, and she said, "No, can you *describe* it?" and every time I said something about it, that it was made of wood or that it was a horse and a man on it, she said, "But can you describe it?"'

'And what happened in the end?'

'She wouldn't give it to me. And then one day, oh, a couple of days later, I saw it on her shelf, and I was sure it was mine, there really wasn't any doubt about it, she'd even admired it beforehand, and there was no one in the corridor and yet, do you know, I couldn't bring myself to take it? I knew it was mine and I couldn't bring myself to take it.'

'I knew girls like that. Angels with dirty mouths. Always legal, everything legal. There are lots of French girls like that. That's what education does for you, you see. You learn to cheat.'

'And yet . . .'

'Yes?'

'The uneducated . . . they frighten me too. They all frighten me.'

'How sad,' the girl said. 'And you are so beautiful.'

'Oh, beauty,' Kate said.

'Really one can describe nothing,' the girl said. 'Isn't that really the truth?'

'You and I,' Kate said. 'It's funny.'

'That's right,' the girl said.

'And now I must go.'

'And be alone,' the girl said, 'why? Please don't.'

'What he's done to us,' Kate said, 'hasn't he? Turning us both into . . . I don't know.'

The girl said, 'Stay with me. Just for a little. Why should we be alone? Why? Even if you hate me.'

'I don't,' Kate said. 'I don't know what I feel. Any more.' She searched the girl's face for her misplaced feelings. 'I only know – I wanted to kill you. It's the only thing I had left I wanted to do. The only positive errand I had left to do. I wanted to kill you. I was almost glad you existed. Now . . .'

'I understand,' the girl said.

'Oh damn you, damn you, you would, you would.' She threw up her arms in a helpless rage. 'You've left me with nothing.'

'No,' the girl said.

'Oh yes, nothing.'

'Poor Kate,' the girl said. 'Poor both of us.'

When Kate threw herself on the girl, she did not know what she would do. 'I still want to,' she said. 'I still want to.' She cried out and her arms were round the girl. She said, 'Oh God.' She spent her passion in weak and inconclusive movements. She fluttered in the girl's arms and could not escape. 'It's absurd,' she said.

'Don't be afraid,' the girl said. 'He loved you. I ought to know.'

Kate looked at her. The girl's face was enlarged with pity and tenderness. Kate kissed the unflinching mouth. She kissed the plain cheeks and came back to that soft mouth which now came to meet her.

'I have to go,' Kate said.

'No,' the girl said. 'You don't have to. Never.'

'You and I,' Kate said. 'You and I. Richard's things!'

22

'Mijo?'

Kate woke at the gentle alarm a milkman sounded. Mijo was asleep. She did not sleep like a girl. She frowned. Her body was heavy on the divan. There was no dream in her. Her flung arms had a demanding boldness.

'Mijo?' Kate bent to the sleeping girl. Mijo shrugged and made an unready mouth at Kate's touch.

She flung herself the other way and the dawn grazed her flesh.

'Mijo?'

Kate was afraid at every sound. Her body still bore the wet and wanton wound of the night.

'Mijo.'

She dressed and turned her back on the road and looked out of the window over the river. The water was a silver sleeve, Elizabethan with pearls.

A cistern sneezed and sneezed and gave way. A door slammed downstairs; a window slid and banged. Silence returned, but solitude was gone. The milkman stopped by the Vitesse.

Kate said, 'Mijo. I must go home.'

Mijo said, 'Oh hullo. There you are.' She frowned at her watch. 'It's early.'

'I thought I'd go before anyone wakes, but ... There're already people about.'

'Nobody will mind.'

'I don't know what to – to – say, to think, I really don't.'

The girl rose from the warm bed. 'I go make us some coffee. O.K.?' Kate shied from her nakedness. 'Nothing to say, nothing to think.' Smiling at Kate with piercing candour, she wrapped herself unhurriedly in an orange robe. 'Is there?'

Kate sat and watched the street. Mijo returned with coffee and a packet of rusks. Kate said, 'I didn't mean – ' The girl put the things on the table and came to where Kate was huddled, forehead against the pane. She put both hands on the older woman's shoulders and looked down at her. Her eyes, in the ordinary light, had a slight squint. Kate was unable to look squarely at her. Yet the girl was looking directly at her. She bent and kissed Kate on either cheek. 'O.K.?' Kate bound her arms round the girl's waist and pulled her to her, but her head flew from side to side of the girl's body in a parody of denial.

'I don't understand,' she said.

Mijo said, 'It's not so surprising, what happened.'

'For you. For me, it's unthinkable.'

'We loved the same man.' Mijo was free and went to pour the coffee. 'It's not so surprising.'

'I cut up your flowers,' Kate said. 'Your freesia. I cut them into pieces.'

'You are very passionate,' the girl said.

'What are we going to do?' Kate said.

The girl cupped her hands round her coffee and seemed to dismiss first one possibility and then another. She put down her cup and stared at Kate. 'No one can help us,' she said. 'No one.' She put her elbows on the table and dropped her chin into her hands. 'So at least there's that.'

23

The phone was ringing in the house. The house was worth a lot of money. Kate had seen from the window of Messrs Warde and Hancock. Now she sat in the Vitesse and considered 14, Oxford Road: detached, tile-hung, with, on the ground floor, three reception rooms, kitchen and breakfast room, w/c and cloakroom. On the first floor four bedrooms, three with handbasins, a bathroom and a separate lavatory. The phone was ringing in the house. And on the second floor a large loft with two dormer windows, at present used for storage, but easily converted into additional bedrooms. It also featured a tower, with intriguing lozenge windows on three sides. The phone was ringing in the house.

There was a mature garden with a variety of shrubs, many of them rare and studiously maintained by the last owner, who was a practising landscape architect, offering direct access to the river. The main-line station was just eight minutes away, with frequent services to Waterloo. There was a good garage and unrestricted parking in the street.

'Hullo.'

'Kate, I've been ringing and ringing.'

'Have you, Mummy? I'm sorry.'

'For the last half hour.'

'I never heard it.'

'Where have you been?'

'They sometimes sound as if they're ringing and they're not ringing the right number at all.'

'I had them check.'

'Well, what would you like me to say? That I knew it was you and I deliberately ignored it?'

'Are we going to this sale or aren't we?'

'Sale. Yes. Why not? We said we would.'

'I haven't had time to get over and view, but it'll do you good to be taken out of yourself.'

The auction was in a large, modern house near Ascot. The drive was too full of cars to please Mrs Sells. She wrinkled her nose, sniffing rivals.

The oak-beamed main room was filled with light from steel-framed windows on two sides. Grilles were drawn across. The auctioneer stood on a travelling pulpit and used his knuckles for a hammer. Mrs Sells sighed and sat down by a small, overcoated man on a buttoned leather Chesterfield.

'Anything?'

The other dealer tasted lemon. 'A certain amount. You see who's here.'

The auction proved a duet between the auctioneer and a grey-haired man who seldom looked up from his catalogue. He simply gestured with his fingers: a club man ordering his usual. Mrs Sells leaned to speak into Kate's ear. 'The Ring,' she said.

'Ring?'

'The Colonel does the buying, the others keep out, and then afterwards –'

'I thought that had been forbidden. I read about it.'

'Nothing's forbidden unless it's done, isn't that right, Mr Singer?'

Mr Singer did not need to answer. He looked with interest at someone as young in the ways of the world as Kate. When Mrs Sells at last made a bid, it was a surprise. Kate found the auctioneer looking in their direction and her mother had her finger up. The grey-haired man glanced up and nodded with apparent politeness at Mrs Sells. The auctioneer took it for a bid, and was right. The piece in dispute was a Jacobean oak sword-chest. The walls of the room were blank where spears and fowling pieces had marked the paint. They were stacked now in bundles, like chimney-sweeps' brushes. Pairs of duelling pistols were displayed on the sword-chest, although they were not part of the lot. Mrs Sells appeared more bored during the bidding in which she was taking part than she had before. It was only ever at the last second that her attention returned to the auctioneer. Each of her bids was telegraphed by a little jolt of the chin. She might have been acknowledging an old enemy. Kate, however, felt the charge of life in her mother's apparent indifference. The Colonel and she played out their sharp courtship through the auctioneer. When Mrs Sells made the final bid, the Colonel bowed, as if his concession to the lady had been deferred only long enough for her to attain the full pleasure of it. 'Too high,' Mrs Sells said.

When the bidding ended, Kate and her mother carried the chest to the Traveller where Bertie was on guard. The chest protruded beyond the tailgate, but Mrs Sells had ropes and sacking to protect it. The merchandise seemed polished and restored by the money which had passed. 'Damn the thing,' Kate said, as the chest budged and the sacking fell.

'Oh she's a beauty. She's a beauty.' Mrs Sells gleamed with her expensive victory. The Colonel saluted her as he made arrangements with his men. 'He didn't quite have it all his own way after all.'

'Couldn't you have made a deal later,' Kate said, 'and saved yourself the trouble?'

'Trouble? That's not trouble. We both knew the game and we played it. That's not trouble.'

'You know,' Kate said, 'I think there's something in this.' They were urging the chest snug in the back of the Traveller. 'Did you look?'

'It was listed "and contents",' Mrs Sells said, 'but

the chest's worth the price, easily, whatever they are. I like those little unknown extras, they're what give the game its sparkle.'

'You never even looked before we loaded it, though. Aren't you curious at all?'

'Highly,' Mrs Sells said, 'but it can always wait.'

'Well, you did me down,' the Colonel said, coming across to them as they tied the last knots. 'You did me down.'

'You were very chivalrous, Petie,' Mrs Sells said. 'My daughter. Colonel Foreshaw.'

'How do you do?' The Colonel was polite enough, but his attention was on Mrs Sells: she might have been the younger woman. 'I'm rarely beaten, and seldom with a good grace, Elizabeth, you know that. You caught me with my bean bag nearly empty, that was all. It's a handsome piece and what's more it's right. I had a thorough recce.'

'I could tell', Mrs Sells said, 'that you had.'

The Colonel said, 'I shall have to keep my eye on you. You're a sight too canny for my peace of mind.'

'The price of putting on speed,' Mrs Sells said. 'Someone is always going to be slipstreaming you.'

'What a lot you know,' the Colonel said.

'It came too late in life to enjoy,' Mrs Sells said.

'You enjoy yourself disgracefully, Elizabeth. We'll have none of your nonsense. Spring comes twice in every year for folk like you. Well, goodnight. Goodnight, Mrs um – Tell me, are you going down to Great Horkesley next week, Elizabeth? Might be worth it. I've dissuaded one or two people.'

'Why weren't you ever a general, Petie?' Mrs Sells said.

'Too crafty,' the Colonel said, and winked at Kate. 'Too crafty, too impatient, and too hard-working.'

'He likes you,' Kate said, as they were leaving.

'He likes a fight,' Mrs Sells said. 'Up to a point.'

24

'You ought to go in with her,' Peter said.

'I'd sooner go in with you,' Kate said.

'I'm glad to hear that,' Peter said. 'Or at least I think I am. And then all along here, by the way, we're planning to put in cherry, almond and peach, which means blossom, once they get a hold, for about six weeks in a year, assuming there isn't too much frost or wind. It's sheltered as you can see.'

'They're quite nice houses.'

'These particular people take a lot of trouble, I will say that for them. They're coining it, of course, but they do give the buyer something for his money, even if it isn't quite enough. Of course they're going for as much as thirty-two grand, most of these new ones, and considering how far we are from Charing Cross, well . . . '

'Who can afford them?' Kate said.

'Anyone who's got one already, roughly speaking. And yet I was over at the first estate they did, or rather the first one of theirs we did – ' An apprehensive slyness burned in Peter Workman's eye. Kate looked away. 'I'm talking about the ones on the old

Deanery Estate and they seemed quite young, for the most part, the tenants: prams and Minis, roughly in that stage. Of course now they're laughing. On an average, those houses have gone up about thirty or forty per cent in a year and a half. Thirty to forty per cent. It makes nonsense of everything. They can afford prams at that rate!'

'And Minis.'

'And Minis. I'll show you inside. Chappie gave me a key, because I like to line up what the landscaping's going to look like from inside as well. No sense in a picture window with a lopsided picture. Funny, the trouble one takes. One tells oneself that there isn't really any good purpose served in worrying about the last crocus and the penultimate daff, and yet one does, one does. For whose benefit, I wonder?'

'Your own, I suppose. Your own satisfaction.'

'Yes, but one's own satisfaction, I mean, what's that when all's said and done?'

'At that point,' Kate said, 'what's anything?'

'They haven't stinted themselves, have they? I suppose it's all to do with wanting to be loved. Double sink, double oven, double double double: how many people really want them? And the land-scaping, our side of the whole thing, in a few years the kids'll probably have snapped off the almonds and the little doggies will have drowned the peaches and dug up the daffs, and yet ... Waste-disposer, you see? I'm surprised they haven't got double loos, quite frankly. Am I boring you?'

'No,' Kate said. 'No.'

'Because we can always go and eat. The upstairs is quite imaginative. Quite a few imaginative touches.'

There was a large room with an open staircase which led up to a gallery. Bedrooms opened off it. The master bedroom had a terrace over the kitchen. They looked down on the ironed site. New trees sprigged the brown earth. In between, a green fuzz was beginning to show, like adolescent beard.

'The architect's drawings showed this terrace lined with geraniums and herbaceous droopies of one kind and another, though whether it will ever happen when people are actually asked to put their hands in their pockets . . . '

'You'll have to come round and sell them,' Kate said.

'Door to door,' Peter said. 'It may come to that, who knows? Kate, I don't suppose this really needs saying, but I wouldn't like to think that I'd never said it. This isn't something sudden, it certainly isn't something – well, I'm not an opportunist, I hope you'll believe me there. I love you. I'm not used to saying things of that kind, especially after all these years, and I don't mean by it what we used to mean then.'

'I know, Peter, I know, I know.'

'By which I mean, it isn't something that's suddenly hit me like a case of measles. I've always admired you and thought the world of you. I never imagined that you'd be interested in me. No, I've put that badly: I never dreamed of, well, taking you away from Richard. Even if I had, I knew very well there wasn't the smallest chance. Richard was my friend. I admired him, I cared for him. If what happened had never happened, I wouldn't have dreamed of saying anything like this to you, although I do have some sort of hope that you might have realized.'

'I understand very clearly,' Kate said, 'and I'm very touched and very grateful.'

'Oh God, I don't want that,' Peter Workman said. 'What I feel about you is pretty straightforward. It's everything else that's complicated and difficult to explain. You see, I feel a bit of a coward, frankly, talking to you like this so soon after Dick's death. I'm afraid of seeming to do something behind his back, but however stupid it seems, I don't actually feel that it's like that at all. Because, you see, I do actually have the feeling – and I know it sounds a bit off – I do actually have the feeling that I'm doing it with his knowledge. I mean, not in an underhand way, in his absence. I believe that if you and I were to, to hit it off, to become what I'd like us to become, Richard would be a part of us. I do actually feel that, regardless of whatever interpretation anyone else might put on it. End of speech. Longest one of my life, longest important one anyway.'

Kate said, 'Dear Peter . . . '

'I'm not asking you to say anything. I'm not asking you to give me an answer, because there really isn't an answer. I'm not honestly asking you to do anything; I'm just trying to tell you something. We're putting in a damned great hedge along there, incidentally, to screen off the service road: instant Dunsinane. I'd feel I'd made an idiot of myself if I'd got myself all ready to talk to you and then said nothing, so there we are. Forgive me?'

'Forgive you?' Kate said. 'Forgive you?'

He stood her against the terrace rail and held the rail either side of her. He leaned and kissed her and she accepted the kiss with a tolerance that he took for encouragement. His second kiss was less grateful; she tolerated it too. She had not been kissed on the mouth by another man since a drunken New Year's Eve when a musician had played to her for some time on a piano in a room a long way from the party.

They went through the empty bedroom, with its row of thin doors in front of built-in cupboards, and down the carpenter's stairs to where sliding windows gave on to a walled patio stocked with provisional plants in black plastic spats.

'Show house,' Peter said. 'Obviously, this one.'

'There'll be people in here shortly,' Kate said. 'Do you think they'll be bothered by our ghosts? Do you think we've left an invisible trail, or a mysterious scent? Perhaps a mysterious scent.'

'Oh I doubt it,' Peter Workman said. 'Don't you have to have been particularly unhappy somewhere if you want to leave a lasting impression?'

'Or murdered,' Kate said.

25

It was dark at last. They had dined at a place near Hampton Court. It had been recommended in the paper. Peter stopped the Cortina in Oxford Road and half turned to Kate. She felt awkward and young. She might have been her own daughter, casting an anxious eye on the dark house in case they were being watched.

Peter said, 'I'm sorry it wasn't a better meal, but of

course it never is. English food doesn't get better, it just gets more expensive.'

'Like England,' Kate said.

'But then where else is there unfortunately? Kate, I only want to say one more thing concerning what I was saying before, and that's please don't think that I only feel what I feel because Mag and I have had this crisis of ours. What I mean is, it isn't something that's been forced on me. I hope this won't seem frightful – '

'Look, Peter, come in, if you want to. We're not fugitives!'

'No, I'll just tell you this. Years ago, when Richard was first courting you, before the long gap when we didn't see each other, we all went out. I don't know whether you ever remember, to a hop, Boat Club thing, at the Grosvenor, do you remember?'

'Good heavens! Was that you? You were with a girl from, don't tell me, from Brazil or somewhere, exotic creature with black hair and a slit skirt up to here – created quite – '

'Is right, is right. Carmen Lardizabal. I used to call her the lard ball, fancy you remembering her!'

'She was very attractive,' Kate said.

'Beautiful, beautiful and a mind like a Cash Register, that girl, take, take, take. Carmen Lardizabal. Anyway, I don't suppose Richard ever told you this, but he and I were in the gents or somewhere, anyway we were on our own, and I was saying what a super girl I thought you were, because a little of Carmen went a very long way I can tell you, olé or no olé, and Richard was saying about how it had reached the point where it was marriage or nothing, as far as you two were concerned – I mean it couldn't go on as it was, for various reasons – and he was doing the usual masculine thing about what a big step it was and how although he was potty about you, he didn't know how he'd feel losing his freedom and all that business, and I said to him, "Dick, I'll tell you one thing, if you don't marry her, I know someone who will and he's standing right next to you at this moment." A week later I saw the engagement in the paper.'

Kate said, 'Thank you for the evening.'

'I'll at least see you to the door. You're not upset, are you? I thought I'd told you that story before, one evening when we were all a bit high, one New Year's Eve once, no?'

'I don't remember,' Kate said.

'Anyway, I don't suppose that was the only reason he married you, to keep you out of my clutches. Carmen Lardizabal! She married the São Paolo branch of quite a decent-sized bank and lived happily ever after. It was all her own vault! Ouch, sorry! Kate, this has been the best evening I personally have had in a long time. I hope it hasn't been too much of a bind from your point of view.'

'It's been nice.'

'At least you don't have to pretend with me,' Peter Workman said. 'There is that to be said.'

Kate opened her door and pushed it for Peter.

'No, I honestly won't. I can see you're about bushed and I've got an early start in the matino. There is something I'd like you to think about though, and that is I've been invited to look at a big project near Geneva; it's another of these residential devvies, but rather a tricky one landscapewise because it's one of these cantilevered jobs and there's always a big problem with soil erosion and landslips – climatic conditions generally – anyway, they want me to go down and take soundings and I wondered quite honestly whether you felt like coming with me. All expenses paid obviously and quite legit, in view of your connection with the firm, always assuming you don't object to being my secretary at least so far as the accounts go.'

'It sounds very tempting,' Kate said. 'Geneva.'

'Not a bad town, if you don't mind walking on other people's gold. I'll let you know if I hear any more.'

Kate said, 'Bless you, Peter.'

'Lonely beds,' Peter Workman said, 'lonely beds.'

Kate was already undressed and the bath was running before she heard his engine start and the car move away from in front of the house. She had not drawn the curtains. Perhaps it had seemed like display, but she had avoided going within his view. She could not, she thought, raise another genial hand that night. She undressed in the bathroom, under the undimmed light. She made no effort to be beautiful in her own eyes. The body she revealed seemed too big for admiration. She was slim and intelligently exercised, but when she saw herself she appeared enormous and white. She might have had the decency, she thought, to shrivel to something more manageable. Who wanted all that flesh? She was in a house too large for herself. She steeped herself in the bath and lost her body under folds of heat, her chin supported by a wimple of water.

The telephone began to ring. She let it ring, listening as attentively as some contestant to puzzling music.

'Yes?'

'Hullo, is that Madame Morris?'

'Mijo! It's you. Is something wrong?'

'Wrong? No. No. I thought perhaps someone else was there, your mother perhaps.'

'No, there's no one. No one at all. Are you all right?'

'Oh yes, of course. What are you doing?'

'I've just had a bath. I'm on my way to bed. What about you?'

'I telephoned earlier, there was no answer.'

'I was out to dinner. An old friend. Well – Peter Workman. I hope you haven't been trying all evening.'

'I came in an hour ago. I thought I would call you.'

'Oh yes? What – what can I do for you? How was your day?'

'When am I going to see you?'

Kate said, 'Mijo, we must be honest with each other.'

'I want to see you very much,' the girl said. 'You blame me, don't you?'

'I'm the older,' Kate said. 'If anyone's to blame ... but I'm afraid I don't think of it like that.'

'On Saturday,' the girl said. 'I am not working. Perhaps we do something.'

Kate said, 'How about the Tate? They generally have something interesting going on. We could go there.'

'O.K.,' the girl said. 'I wish it was last night.'

Kate sat on the bed and went on drying herself.

'And we were together.'

Kate said, 'I'll call for you, shall I, on Saturday? What time?'

The girl said, 'I miss you.'

Kate said, 'About eleven o'clock, how would that be for you?'

'Oh make it earlier, if you like. Ten o'clock.'

'Half past,' Kate said. 'I'll see you at half past ten.'

'O.K. And I keep the whole day,' the girl said.

Kate put down the telephone at last. Richard had the telephone his side. She stood up and moved her head here and there, as if she had forgotten something and was trying, by looking at one thing after another, to find a clue to what it might be.

26

She twisted the key and killed the engine. The car rolled up to the front of the girl's digs. There had been a heavy shower. The trees, pollarded to neatness, dripped on to the car. Heavy drops, without the rhythm of a proper storm, plopped on to the windscreen in soft stars and ran down into the rubber. The clink of them falling on to the roof was flat and pointless; Kate remembered Bryan Morris drumming his nails. She sat in the car and watched Mijo's window.

The girl was wearing her yellow P.V.C. coat and coal-scuttle hat. She made a bad face at the weather, but then grinned and came wagging down the garden, knees together, feet thrown out, one hand unnecessarily on her head.

'How are you?'

'I'm all right. Get in. It's going to start again.'

'June, I must say, even in England I expected better. Well? Am I all right like this?'

'I like you in that. I liked you in it before.'

'Army surplus,' the girl said. 'Or so they say. Perhaps just surplus. *Bonjour.*' She used the convention to kiss Kate on either cheek. 'We don't have to go anywhere, you know, if you don't want to.'

'Oh, I think we should,' Kate said.

The Tate had an exhibition by a man who painted only maps. Some of them were blow-ups. The names of villages and houses were spelled out, although often there was not room for the full word. Other of the pictures, however, were of sections of contour maps, or of special maps which depicted rainfall or cultivation. Several of them had been exactly repeated, so far as form went, but with different colours. The selection of colours seemed each time to provide a new reading, a new climate, a new scale. The two women stood closer together in front of some than of others. At times they separated. Once Mijo split off into another room, outside the special exhibition. Kate looked round the imaginary maps and the girl was no longer there. She was held by a kind of arbitrary impotence; she could not bring herself to follow. She knew where Mijo had gone and soon she saw her, in the next room but one, standing with her hands on her hips. Although her face was averted, she could imagine the jut-chinned familiarity with which she was contemplating a Bonnard. A young man, with a beard like an advertisement, circled and approved of the picture Mijo was admiring, or of the picture Mijo made. It was curious, the mixture of pride and anguish with which Kate saw the girl brush off the bearded boy and return to her.

'Let's eat before the rush,' Kate said. 'What do you think?'

'I don't mind when I eat.'

Kate dreaded the bodies. Mijo was wearing a studiedly plain expression. Kate took the surliness for a compliment: Mijo let the world see her dull and forbidding and then, as they went down the cold steps to the restaurant, she shot Kate a look of brazen candour. She went wide to the far wall and then back. 'I want to go to Mexico,' she said. 'One day, I want to go to Mexico and climb the pyramids.'

'Pyramids? In Mexico?'

'Oh yes, of course. How else would you call them? The Mayan temples, with all the steps. The first man I ever loved told me about them.'

'Was he a Mexican?'

'French. Diplomatic. His father was in the diplomatic; he was a boy there. You've seen them, surely, with all the steps going up?'

'Yes, of course,' Kate said, 'in, in – '

'Yucatan. They are very steep, you know; the tourists get dizzy. The Mexicans, people who are used to them, they can go up and down without difficulty, like running up and down stairs, but the tourists, they have to have chains to hold on to, to avoid the vertigo. Once you get used to something, it is nothing, but until then – people fall, you know, he used to tell me, even standing still.'

Only a few tables were occupied. They took their trays to a corner empty except for a grey couple sitting at a bare table. The woman had put their cups behind them and was writing cards.

'Why does one always watch other people?' Kate said.

'What people?'

Kate indicated. The man was doing a crossword in the paper. The woman finished her cards and looked round the room; then she took a corner of the paper and bent it up to read the underneath. She needed her other glasses. When she had found them, she bent up more and more of the page. The man took the paper from her and used one of her postcards to make a margin along which he tore the corner with the crossword. He then handed the rest of the paper to her. Kate and Mijo reached for each other and leaned together, smuggling laughter between them like a forbidden pet.

Kate said, 'Did you really understand those pictures? The maps, did you really understand what he was getting at?'

'I don't know,' the girl said.

'Oh thank goodness,' Kate said, 'because I didn't either. I looked at them and looked at them but I didn't really know what I was supposed to be looking at. I suppose we should have bought the catalogue. What was the significance of the particular places, did you work that out at all?'

'Not one little tiny bit,' the girl said. 'Do you think it matters?'

'I'll tell you exactly what I think,' Kate said, 'I don't think it matters in the smallest. But I'm always afraid other people will know things. I thought you'd have all the answers.'

'Not at all,' the girl said. 'I don't even have questions.'

'Oh I'm so glad,' Kate said. 'Now I shall be able to eat. You know I sometimes still dream about exams, do you ever? I dream that I'm back at college and I'm going into an exam and I don't even know what it's going to be in. All I know is that I should have prepared myself for it and I absolutely haven't. Does that ever happen to you?'

'I think he paints maps because he likes to paint maps. A painter can paint anything, that's the thing about painters. Anything or nothing. The idea of a subject doesn't seem to interest them any more. It only interests subjects. At least that is what a painter told me once.'

'I'm always afraid I'm missing something.'

'Oh you,' the girl said, 'you're always afraid of everything. Why are you?'

'There's always something between me and what I want.'

'Perhaps that's what you want,' the girl said.

'Oh that's too convenient. That's too pat.'

'Is there at the moment?'

Kate said, 'No. That's what's so lovely. And so frightening. You see?'

27

'Why are you frightened? Of what?'

'Of so many things you'll laugh.'

'Then let me laugh,' the girl said.

'Of love,' Kate said, and the girl did not laugh. 'Of this. Of what's happened. Of everything. Do you think I don't mean it?'

'I'm here,' Mijo said.

'Yes, and I'm frightened of that too.'

'You have never made love with a woman before?'

'Never. Good heavens! Never.'

'You are ashamed. You think it wrong?'

'Wrong? I don't know. Astonishing. Ruinous, only I don't know of what. Have you done it so often?'

'Not at all,' the girl said.

'How do you manage to be so calm?'

'Why are you going away from me?'

'Oh because . . . I don't know.'

'I feel so comfortable with you,' the girl said.

'That's because you're sure of me,' Kate said.

'Not at all, not at all! Not in the least. That's the last thing.'

Kate said, 'Did you lock the door?'

'No one will come. No one will find you. You are afraid!'

'I told you.'

'Mrs Morris,' the girl said.

'I don't know what I am. I feel I have no ground to stand on. No right to – to resist, to deny anything. I feel as if I could be arrested, raped, I don't know, anything, and I couldn't do anything about it.'

'No one ever can,' the girl said. 'Can they?'

'Oh that's too easy,' Kate said, 'that's too glib.'

'Glib.'

'Yes, it comes too easily off the tongue, an idea like that. I'm English, I don't ever remember feeling that just anything could happen and there was nothing I could do about it.'

'It's a birth,' the girl said, and kissed Kate on the mouth and left her lips against the other woman's, eyes too close for seeing. 'You understand me?'

'I love you,' Kate said, 'and I don't know what that means or where it will end either.'

'You are serious,' the girl said. 'Like him. Will it end?'

Kate drew herself apart from the girl and braced herself against the back wall behind the narrow divan. 'I must go.'

'Have you always been afraid?' the girl said. 'I believe you've always been afraid. It is not something new.'

'I don't know. Perhaps.'

'You want always to be dressed,' the girl said. 'Isn't that right?'

'No, no.'

'When you are with a lover. Afterwards, you want always to be dressed.'

'I was never with a lover before,' Kate said.

'Richard?' the girl said.

'I was never like that,' Kate said. 'What makes you think so? What makes you say a thing like that?'

The girl did not answer. She sat studying Kate.

'Mijo?'

It was a staring game.

'Answer me.'

The girl shook her head, denying tenderness. She shook her head and dared Kate to move. She might have been teaching. She dared Kate; she wanted her to endure that painful silence and Kate could believe, even as she trembled, that the girl wanted it for her sake. There was something she had to learn.

'There's nothing beyond us,' the girl said. 'No one else judges us, no one else can hurt us. No one will come in and if they do, they will be nothing. There are no reports.'

Kate said, 'Oh come, for you, perhaps. I have another life.'

The girl shook her head.

'You're trying to rob me,' Kate said, 'to take something from me.'

The girl held her as she cried out. The girl held her and looked over her through the windows to where the last of the sun was strong on the branchless trees. Kate fought free and threw her arms up around her own head to cut off the light. She wrestled herself into the corner where she huddled; dressed in her own arms. From below came the sudden sound of children. The children brought Kate away from her corner.

'You can never tell whether they're crying or laughing,' she said. 'People never know, I sometimes think, whether they choose to play with people who make them laugh or with people who make them cry.'

'Or which they want when they choose whatever they have chosen. They're laughing. They are actually laughing.'

'Did he often speak of me then?' Kate said.

'Oh! Too often,' the girl said, 'too often! I used to be very tired of you.'

'Once when I was at school –'

'Oh what a long time you spent at that school!'

'Yes, I overheard some girls talking about another

one in the art room. They spoke so coldly of her, so dispassionately, not at all nastily, certainly not altogether nastily anyway, but in so casual a tone, as though she had no particular importance one way or another, they said she was intelligent, but rather too careful, they said she was a bad loser, even though she was a good player – I can't even remember the game – and that she wasn't somebody you could rely on, even though she was very friendly. I remember especially one of them said, and it was the tone that struck me, it was horribly contemptuous, "Oh," she said, "nothing will ever be quite good enough for madam!" They were talking about me.'

'Of course,' said the girl.

'I didn't recognize myself. You see, I don't think I ever bothered to sit back and analyse myself. They said I was intelligent; I think I was only clever. I was clever. I could do anything that I was set, but I never questioned the questions. Have you ever heard people talking about you?'

'No,' Mijo said. 'No.'

'I avoided those two girls for days. I felt robbed of myself. I was quite empty. As I felt, as I felt when this all happened: Richard. I felt I had been – what? – ransacked. Bill once wrote ramsacked, I remember, in a school essay. The town had been ramsacked, with an m –'

'I know.'

'Very expressive, I suppose. Sometimes –' Kate caught the girl looking up at her. 'I wanted to prove them wrong,' she said, 'I became quite deliberately capricious. I was late for lessons. I didn't do my prep. My form mistress wanted me to go to the doctor. I looked at the two girls, who of course had no idea I'd overheard their conversation and had probably forgotten it themselves, and I tried to convey to them how wrong they had been, without, of course, admitting that I was aware of them at all. Oh the complexities of trying to live in other people's eyes!'

'I was going to say.'

'Which is why I did. Have you never done that?'

'Only by being French,' the girl said.

Kate said, 'You seem so certain always.'

'We are not so romantic,' the girl said. 'Certainty is our only form of doubt.'

'That's rather clever.'

'I didn't say it,' the girl said.

'Who did?'

'Oh, the diplomat as a matter of fact.'

28

'It was all girls this school of yours?'

'All girls,' Kate said. 'In the country.'

'And yet you never – '

'Never,' Kate said. 'Never. We were very innocent. We didn't know anything. I don't even particularly remember ever wanting anything. It was the war partly, I think. Richard always said sex was deliberately cut out of our diet. Put on the ration anyway.'

'Oh la,' the girl said. 'Now, what shall we eat?'

They had gone to the supermarket to shop for their evening meal. The girl bought ready-made things, but she chose carefully. Kate deferred to her; they might have been abroad. Kate caught sight of her own face in a mirror behind the poultry. She was shocked by the joy she saw in it. Mijo had gone for cheese.

She was talking to a tall, long-haired man with gold-rimmed glasses who wore a grey and black djellabah. She pressed the Camemberts one after another, regardless of the notice, while she chatted with the young man. When Mijo touched the young man's shoulder goodbye and turned in search of her, Kate managed to be choosing an avocado.

'Josh,' the girl said.

'Josh?'

'I was talking to. We are all in and out of here all the time. He calls us food junkies; the bedsitter fixers, you know?'

'I didn't notice him,' Kate said. 'Which one is he?'

'He's gone now. He was here. You didn't see me talking to him?'

'No,' Kate said. 'I don't think so. Is he a particular friend of yours?'

'Not at all. I don't like him much at all. He is very skinny and very young.'

'You don't like young men?'

'I like them sometimes, but he is very skinny, you know, and he doesn't wash his hair. I like men to be clean.'

As they were walking back to the house, Kate said, 'Have you had a lot of young men?'

'As opposed to what?'

'Not as opposed to anything. Lovers. Men. Have you had a lot?'

'No, absolutely not. No. Serious or not serious?'

'They all seem serious to me,' Kate said. 'Or not, I suppose.'

'Richard was your first man really?'

'Yes,' Kate said. 'Is that something to be ashamed of?'

'Suppose we had not known what we were supposed to do and say, suppose we had had no idea,' the girl said. 'Think how happy we could have been, the three of us! These things you discover always too late!'

'Happy? I don't know. Could we? And where would Bill have fitted in? And everything else.'

'Men like the idea of two women,' the girl said.

'Do they?'

'Did you never talk of things like that?'

'We talked about everything,' Kate said. 'Shall I lock the door? It was locked before.'

'Do you think if a man came home and found his wife and mistress making love he would be angry, or shocked, or jealous? I don't think so. I think it would be a dream come true!'

'Is that what one wants of dreams?' Kate said.

'Midge? Did you get any katsup? I forgot like a damned fool. There's always one stupid thing. Oh, I'm sorry. I'm sorry!'

'Oh Josh, this is, this is Mrs Morris.'

'Kate Morris,' Kate said.

'Hi. Sorry, I didn't realize. I assumed –'

'You should never assume,' the girl said.

'My morals need a lot of attention,' Josh said. 'I have to do something about it. Meantime, do you have any katsup?'

'Of course.'

When Josh had gone, Kate said, 'I thought the French never used ketchup.'

'Are you kidding?'

'I thought they never used "kidding" either!'

'Are you kidding?' The girl stood with her hands on her hips, a fresh and mocking smile on her young face. 'Don't you know the original jackdaw came from Rheims? We pick up everything.'

'So it seems,' Kate said.

The girl ambled up to her and put her arms round her neck to be kissed. Kate did not respond immediately; the girl had to reach, on tiptoe, to press the kiss. For a moment Kate thought that she was indifferent. Then her arms were round the girl.

'Easy,' the girl said. 'Easy, my darling.'

'Mijo, I'm going to go now.'

The girl watched this announcement as if it were something else, a new expression in the other woman, not an intention. She held Kate in her arms. 'You still want to hurt me,' she said.

'I don't want to hurt either of us.'

'You want to hurt me,' the girl said.

'I can't stay. How can I stay? If I'm not at home, people will wonder where I am.'

'What people?'

'Friends. Everyone.'

'Peter Workman.'

'Does your friend from below always walk in like that, without knocking?'

'Friend? Oh, Josh! He did knock.'

'He also walked in.'

'He pops in. He's a bit like that. He's been smoking maybe.'

'Smoking? Pot, you mean.'

'Maybe; it makes him forget.' She left Kate where she was and went and twisted the French lock. 'Better? He did once come in at the wrong moment rather.'

Kate said, 'Will you ever marry, do you think?'

'Why do you ask me? I have no reason not to.'

'You think it can work, do you, that's what I mean?'

'You mean, will I dare after what I have done?'

'No.'

'Yes, my darling, you do mean that. It's funny, people who think they know what is right and wrong, they always think they have no need to tell the truth.'

'I must go,' Kate said, 'truly.'

'Who are these friends? Are they people you really care about?'

'I do have friends,' Kate said. 'Strange as it may seem.'

'I want you to stay,' the girl said.

'Because you want me to,' Kate said, 'or because I don't want to?'

'Because when I am with you – do you like to hear me say it, is that why you ask?'

'I like to hear you say anything,' Kate said.

'Well then, because if you are here, when you are here, there is still some warmth. There is still some life. There. Some hope. Something.'

'I love you,' Kate said, and she was hurrying to find her bag and anything else that might incriminate her.

'You fear it though, don't you, what you feel?'

'Of course. Yes, I do. Of course, I do.'

'You're afraid to let go,' the girl said. 'Abandon. You fear abandon.'

Kate laughed. 'We once queued for a cinema years

ago. It was supposed to be the story of an Abandoned Woman. It was before anyone ever appeared without their clothes on and this woman was supposed to be naked on the screen. Richard wanted to see it. And the nearest it got was a close-up of a nude portrait, a very decorous nude portrait that this abandoned woman had had painted of her. So whenever anyone talks about abandon ... I had another glove. I had another glove somewhere.'

The girl said, 'Maybe I find it later.'

'You haven't taken it, seriously, have you? Hidden it or something? Because that would be so silly.'

'When I clean up the room. Always on Sunday morning I clean up the room. You never slept with another man?'

'Does that shock you?' Kate said. 'I come from a very conventional background. And a conventional foreground too, if it comes to that. I married when I was twenty-two, why should I ever have slept with anyone else?'

'And you waited till you were married?'

'No, of course not. Before we went to bed? No, of course not.'

'You did not hesitate?'

'Oh, I hesitated!'

'Until he had promised,' the girl said. 'Right?'

'I know what you're trying to do,' Kate said. She sat down and bent to look under the shadows of the furniture.

'Stay with me,' the girl said.

'Mijo, I'm going home.'

'Stay with me,' the girl said, 'and then go. If you still want to.'

'Not tonight,' Kate said.

'Is tonight something special? Something I don't know?'

'All that's special is that I said I was going to go and I must.'

'And tomorrow then? Shall I see you? Or ... ?'

Kate picked the glove off the shelf behind the books and stood up. She saw it only as she stood up, yet standing seemed to follow the find.

'You don't go to church?'

'Church! I haven't been to church since – ' She thrust the glove into her bag and snapped it shut.

'I know!' the girl said. 'Tomorrow I come to see you. Then if your friends telephone, everything is quite normal. O.K.?'

'I was thinking of Bill, my son, he usually phones.'

'I come on my bicycle. It's good for the figure. You should get one. We could go places together.'

'Midge!' Kate said.

29

She stopped in Oxford Road. She had taken to leaving the car in the street. Otherwise she had to get out and open the gate and then get in again and drive into the garage, reclose the gates, close the garage. It had been all right when there were two of them.

It was dark, but there were lights in houses. The occasional car drove by. People called out 'Terrific evening.' There was a party in the road. As she glanced up at her own house, she was surprised by a flash in the bedroom window. A passing car must have lent it the illusion of life.

The front door was locked. It was on the chain. She could not get in. She frowned, but she felt no alarm. Mrs Jenkins had perhaps been in to leave something, or take something, and she could have slipped the chain across and then gone out the back. Kate had the kitchen key with her, so she went down between the garage and the fence.

Someone was in the house. She heard the creak of the landing board Richard was always promising to nail. It meant taking up the carpet and he never got round to it. The board creaked. There was life in the house. She trembled, but she was not afraid.

'Who's there?'

The silence creaked. He had gone into her bedroom.

'Richard, darling,' she called out in a loud voice. 'Darling, do come; someone's here.'

She acted as though she expected his strong reply. She allowed him time to lock the garage.

'Richard . . . ' She pushed his name ahead of her, like a real person, up the stairs. The bedroom door was ajar. She pushed it open. He was outlined, like a hard ghost, against the window by the dressing-table. He was bending to open it, but now he turned and she heard his voice.

'Don't touch that light. You stay where you are.'

She sniffed. There was a beastly smell.

She said, 'What're you doing? What are you doing in my house?'

'I'm in the wrong house,' he said. 'I made a mistake.'

'The wrong house? You expect – '

'I don't expect anything. I'm on my way. I'm going. Don't try to stop me and there won't be any trouble.'

'That window's been stuck for years,' Kate said.

The telephone began to ring.

The man said, 'What the hell are you doing?'

'Doing? Nothing. I didn't do anything. It's the phone.'

'Leave it. Just leave it. I'm going down the stairs and then I'm going out, O.K.? Now all you have to do is stand aside and let me pass. That's all you have to do, not get in my way. Sod that bloody phone. Now don't you go and get in my way.'

He began to walk towards her.

'You smell,' she said, 'you're filthy, you're dirty. How dare you come into my house? How dare you come into my house?'

He sidled past her and she was soiled by his fear. She flew at him. She grabbed him by the ear and the hair and shook him and banged him against the door. She kicked at his shins.

'Insect,' she said, 'insect.'

'I told you not to,' he said. 'I warned you.' She sensed that he was offended. He whined. 'Get off. Stop it. Stop it.'

She could not stop. She kicked at him like the embers of a fire. He was a threat to her house. She kicked and fought and goaded him to fight her. He had a suitcase with him. He had a suitcase. He pushed her with his spare hand and she knocked against the telephone on the bedside table. She snatched it off its hook and realized from its cawing that the ringing had already stopped.

He said, 'You'd better not,' and grabbed the receiver and pulled. He got more flex. He reeled it over his fist and jerked the telephone on to the carpet.

'Put down that case,' she said. 'Put it down. That's mine. That's not yours. That's mine.'

He put it down and threw her on to the bed, two-handed now. She kicked out, like a girl. He caught at her feet. Her shoe came off. She yelled at him and he jumped to stifle her and they wrestled on the bed. He made no effort to punch her. He fought her to get away. She might have been a door which opened the wrong way. He put his weight against her to keep her where she was while he passed. Her gasps and blurted abuse made him mutter, 'Stop it, be quiet, stop it.' His hand was over her mouth. 'Please.' She pushed him away with all her force and she was off the bed and up to the light and in a flash she was in the room with a man.

He was quite tall and slim, with short, dark hair and the kind of regular features that once sold things on hoardings. He looked no more than thirty, but a dated thirty. He wore a tweed sports jacket and grey flannel trousers and shoes with laces. He stood there long enough (he actually straightened his green and yellow paisley tie) for her to have full sight of him. Then he was running past her, as if they were both accidental victims of some common emergency. He ran to the light and turned it out and kept his hand over the switch and his breathing was that of a rescuer just in time. 'You bloody fool, why do that? What do you want me to do? Eh? I'm going. I'm going. I told you.'

'You bastard,' she said, 'you fucking bastard, you fucker, you fucker, you fucker.' She tore him back into the room and he nearly fell, unbalanced by the suitcase he had taken up once again. He tried to pull away. Her clothes seemed tangled with him. He ripped something as he moved.

'I don't want any trouble,' he said. 'Look, stop it –'

He flung her from him and was lurching round the bed while she threw things. She threw the Venetian jars and the tortoiseshell dressing set. She threw whatever she could find. He fought the door like a second enemy and finally she threw herself. He started to hit out. She felt his fist in her belly and then a stinging blow on the ear and she cried out, as if at last she had got what she was after.

'Let me go, will you, you stupid cow? Let me go.' She had him by the trousers. She was trying to get her knee into him. He thrust the case into her and was gone across the landing. She ran with the case and toppled it over the banisters. He reeled and fell against the flower prints and crashed a comic few steps down to the hall. The case burst and things exploded over him.

'Take it all, you bastard, you swine, you cheat, you trickster, you bastard, take it. You packed it. You wanted it. Clear it all up and take it, you swine. Go on. You wanted it, take it.'

He was pulling and pulling at the door.

'You did it, you fool, you imbecile, you did it. The chain, you idiot.'

'I'm sorry,' he said.

'Sorry! Sorry? You idiot, you cheap fool. Don't you want it, aren't you going to take it after all this?'

'I want out,' the man said. 'That's all I want.'

'Why did you come? If you don't want anything, why did you come?'

'I don't want a thing. I want out.' The man wrestled the nippled tongue from its guard and undid the chain. He ran away. The door banged behind him.

Kate called out. 'You shit, you shit, you shit. You filthy shit. You dirty man. You pig.' Her voice lost its strength. She spoke in a clear tone, as though there were someone close. 'You come here and then you go and you leave things just anywhere, you don't care, you think you can just walk out and leave things it doesn't matter where. You call yourself a man. You're a pig. You're a bastard. You're a shit. Fucker,' she said. 'Fucker.' She could have been reading the word on a wall for the first time. It crossed her lips like a new taste. 'Fucker. He was a fucker.'

Nothing was damaged of the things in the case. They were a mixture of Richard's things and hers, and theirs. Her fur cape; his dinner jacket and trousers; a Florentine jewellery box (including a cameo he had given her when Bill was born, and a heart-shaped locket when Erica was); the silver they never used, out of its canteen; a bottle of scotch and half of vodka; the clock from the kitchen and her alarm from beside the bed; a transistor of Bill's that had not worked for ages; the toaster and enough odd clothes to avoid a rattle. Kate took the jewellery (she had never worn the locket) and left the other things where they were.

The photograph of Richard in naval uniform, on her bedside table, had been knocked over. The glass was broken. The photograph was naked: a man without his spectacles. The unprotected face of the print was blind against her fingers. She picked out triangles of glass and dropped them into the waste basket. She managed to cut herself. She drowned the cut under the tap and then she went and sat on the stairs, amid the scattered belongings, and sucked her fingers. She might have been waiting for someone to come back. From time to time she said a few words.

30

She watched the girl through the dimpled glass of the front door as she came up the path. She heard the gate and the ticking of a wheeled bicycle and then the first few discs darkened with the girl's shadow. The door was alive with her approach. Her image ran quick as a stain across the glass. She filled the right-hand panel and spilled into the left as her face tipped a pool of pink on to the surface. She rang and pressed a darker face against the glass. Kate sat on the stairs and watched the liquid image of the girl tilt from one side to the other as she sought to see.

Kate said, 'I'm coming,' and sat on the stairs. The girl bent down. She was gone. The glass was clear. The letter-box flap came open behind its wire muzzle.

'It's me. Mijo.'

Kate opened the door.

'I've brought the booze!' the girl said. She had prepared a joke: a milk bottle in each hand. She said, 'Darling, what's happened?' She put the bottles inside the door and swung her tote bag in after them. She shut the door and took Kate by the arms and scanned her face. 'Darling, tell me.'

'I had a visitor,' Kate said.

'You look awful. You look terrible. When?'

'Last night. When I got home. I'm fine.'

The contents of the suitcase still littered the hall and the stairs.

'I'm perfectly all right now.'

'I don't think so. I don't think so. You haven't been in those clothes all night?'

'Yes,' Kate said. 'I do seem to.'

'You've been in your clothes all night and you say you're all right? You're going straight to bed.'

Kate laughed. 'Oh Mijo . . .'

'You're hurt. Darling, your face. What kind of a visitor?'

'The uninvited kind,' Kate said.

'A thief,' the girl said. 'You've had a thief.'

'He didn't take anything,' Kate said. 'Can you be a thief if you don't take anything?'

'He hit you.'

'I hit him,' Kate said.

'Did you call the police?'

'I didn't want them. I didn't want them.'

'You've got concussion,' the girl said.

'Oh Mijo,' Kate said, and began to laugh or cry. 'I don't know.'

'Please now, you go upstairs and get into bed and I bring you something.'

'A present?'

'Some tea. With tea in it! Please. Do as I say.'

'Do as you say,' Kate said. 'And what if I don't?'

'I call the police myself. You go upstairs and I clear up the mess.'

'Throw it all away,' Kate said.

When Mijo came with the tea, Kate was sitting on the bed with the broken picture in her hands.

'Do you know,' Kate said, 'the car is still in Ipswich? The Alvis. It's still in Ipswich.'

'One day we go and get it,' the girl said, 'but not today. Today we do nothing. Today we rest. I think you should call the police, I'm serious.'

'No,' Kate said. 'I don't want anyone strange in my house. How can I answer questions? How can I have them here?'

'There's someone now,' the girl said.

A car had stopped.

Kate said, 'Why? What's happened? What did you do?'

'It's probably one of those famous friends of yours.'

Kate said, 'You stay up here. Please, you stay here. I'll go down.'

'Let them ring.'

'Mijo, please, please do as I say, please. Stay here until I say.'

It was Peter Workman. He wore his children on either hand.

'We're on our way to the cricket,' he said. 'And it suddenly occurred to us you might feel like coming. Up on the heath.'

'Peter, I can't.'

'I did actually call you last night. Not about this, but I did actually call. You must've been busy.'

'Yes,' Kate said. 'I'm not actually all that much of a cricket enthusiast.'

Peter said, 'Kate, is everything all right?'

She said, 'You go on, you go on.'

'You look tremendous,' Peter Workman said. 'It's just – you look really tremendous. Are you sure – ?'

'I'm just having a sort out,' Kate said. 'I'm sure I look absolutely dreadful.'

'Not to me. We really were hoping you'd come, weren't we, Val? Have you taken up cycling?'

'Cycling? Oh! Oh no, no, that belongs to somebody else. Somebody's helping me to get straight.'

Peter said, 'Well chaps, it seems we're off. Perhaps I'll give you a ring. Perhaps tonight? Or I might drop by.'

'Oh I wish you would,' Kate said, 'but not tonight.'

She shut the front door and put the chain across. Then she went into the sitting-room. Perhaps the thief had been leaving it till last. It was undisturbed. She sat down and looked at an old paper. The landing board creaked. She put down the paper and went to the door and listened.

'Kate?'

She leaned her head against the jamb.

'Kate?'

She said, 'Don't come down.'

'They've gone surely?'

'Just stay there,' Kate said.

She walked into the hall and looked up the stairs.

She said, 'Mijo.'

'Yes? I'm here. Are you all right?'

She said, 'Mijo?'

'Are you coming?'

She said, 'Please get into my bed.'

'You're not well,' the girl said. She came and leaned over the balustrade. Kate was standing by the hall table. She made no effort to conceal herself, but her voice was that of someone out of sight.

'I'm perfectly well. I want you to do what I say. Will you?'

'Yes,' the girl said. 'I will, but – '

'Then please get into my bed.'

'Kate? Are you coming?'

The girl's clothes were on the chair. Kate picked up each garment and folded it. Then she took off her own clothes and stood in the centre of the carpet. The girl held the bedclothes to her chin. Kate walked to the bed and sat on it, on Richard's side, by the door, and drew down the sheet and the blanket and embraced the girl. 'All day,' she said. 'All all day.'

31

'Darling,' the girl said. She muffled Kate with her body. There was no sound in the house. It was like a midnight, the sun full on the windows. Kate caressed the line of dark hairs on the girl's back. On the bedside table was the broken frame with Richard's picture. Kate's left hand felt over the surface of the table. She found an icicle of glass. It seemed to soften under her fingers.

She said, 'I cut myself last night.'

'Did you, darling?'

'On some broken glass.'

'You're bruised, I know,' the girl said. 'I saw. I felt. Did I hurt?'

'I love you,' Kate said.

The girl said, 'Sleep, darling, why don't you sleep?'

'Are you tired?'

'Darling, I'm tired, yes.'

'Then you sleep. I'm going to get some food,' Kate said. 'I'm going to go down and make us something.' She measured the glass between finger and thumb. She took the splinter and laid it on the girl's back.

'What are you doing?'

'Can't you feel?'

The girl wrinkled her back: one shoulder blade and then the other rose and settled. 'You're tickling. What is it, darling?'

Kate pointed the fragment and held it upright. The girl sat up. 'What are you doing?' Kate kissed her breast and slipped out of the bed. At the abrupt movement, the fragment of glass had fallen from the girl's back. It was somewhere in the bed. 'Cover yourself,' Kate said. 'Snuggle down.'

'I wanted to get something for you, darling,' the girl said.

'No.' Kate bent over the girl and kissed her forehead and took the hair from her eyes. 'You're going to stay here, and I'll bring you something.'

'I want to come down,' the girl said.

'Tomorrow you have to work,' Kate said.

The girl put her arms up to Kate's neck. 'Why are you being so nice? You're being so nice.'

'Because I love you,' Kate said. 'You make yourself comfortable.'

32

'Darling, I ought to go,' the girl said.

'It's still early,' Kate said. 'I'll take you later, if you want me to. I'll take you in the car.'

'I have things I have to do,' the girl said.

'I don't think you should do anything else today at all. What do you have you must do?'

'Some washing,' the girl said. 'Things like that.'

'Washing? I thought everyone took their washing to the laundromat?'

'Are you afraid, darling?'

'Afraid? Afraid of what?'

'Your thief,' the girl said.

'Oh him. I don't think he'll come back. No, I'm not afraid.'

'Then – ?'

'Bill's home next week,' Kate said. 'Half term.'

'Will I not see you?'

'Oh I don't suppose he'll stick around the house exclusively. He's probably bringing someone. I'll phone you.'

'A girl?'

'I assume. One never knows for certain. They're so changeable at his age. Sometimes they want a girl and then at others . . . '

'You mean . . . ?'

'Oh no, nothing like that. Good heavens! He's very keen on girls, it's just that sometimes he goes off the whole idea, becomes a baby again, or at least a young boy, and all he wants is to muck about, as he puts it. Kick a ball, listen to records, have endless awful fry-ups.'

'Will you tell him anything?'

'He's not interested in what happens to me,' Kate said. 'Anyway I don't tell people things.'

'What do you tell yourself?' the girl said. 'About us?'

Kate said, 'Was it – was it very physical, your thing? With Richard. Or – ?'

The girl said, 'You know what kind of man he was.'

'I've never seen any of your work. Your design work. He obviously admired it. He obviously thought you were very talented. I mean, to take you on a trip like the one he did. And I don't suppose it was the first.'

'No,' the girl said, 'it wasn't.'

'You often went with him.'

'Occasionally. I wasn't there that long.'

Kate said, 'How did he make the first approach?'

'You mean, how did he – ?'

'Yes,' Kate said. 'You know what I mean.'

'It was through work. You're right: he liked some of the things I did. I was alone in London, at the time. I worked hard. And late sometimes. I was available.'

Kate put her arm round the girl. 'I believe you.'

'We would be alone sometimes, working, naturally. He was nice to me. I began to like him because he was nice to me. And then he liked to talk over a problem, to discuss ideas. You know how it is.'

'One thing led to another,' Kate said.

'He had a very easy way of talking, very frank, very

honest. I liked that. He looked you in the eyes and he really tried to communicate. He was not at all like a Frenchman.'

'What's a Frenchman like?'

'A Frenchman makes an appeal to you which is – I don't know how to explain exactly – which is somehow general. Do you know what I mean? He assumes something. He avoids the personal. Love is not something personal for him. A Frenchman makes love into something moral.'

'Moral?'

'He gets a girl by making her feel that it is her duty to be his mistress. There is a very precise way of announcing each stage. It is very moral. You refuse to sleep with him – you are behaving childishly, you are immature, you are naïve, you are dishonest. Dick was never like that at all. He was very personal. May I tell you something?'

'Yes,' Kate said. 'I wish you would.'

'I don't think I should perhaps.'

'Oh Mijo, Mijo, not that old game – '

'The first time he kissed me . . . '

'Go on.'

'It meant nothing. I had had an idea. For a lay-out. A very simple idea. As a matter of fact, it wasn't originally my idea at all. It was something the first man I worked for had done to a house belonging to a rather famous conductor actually and I suggested it for a project Dick was working on at the time. He kissed me, you know.'

'Congratulations.'

'Exactly. Congratulations. And then, well, he kissed me again.'

'Congratulations,' Kate said.

'It was nice. It was generous. He was pleased. Until then, there had been nothing. He was not one of those. Anyway, that was it.'

'That's not what you were going to tell me,' Kate said. 'You were going to tell me something else.'

The girl said, 'Oh, darling, these things . . .'

'He preferred you to me. He told you it was better with you than it had ever been with me, is that what you want to tell me?'

The girl said, 'The end of the next day he kissed me again. He had waited all day.'

'You'd waited all day as well, presumably.'

'Then he said, "Last night I loved my wife –" because I had not even met you, I think, at that point – "last night," he said, "I loved my wife more than I have loved her for many years." He meant between you in bed there had been something, I think, that night. He wanted to tell me, this is the point, that whatever we had done or might do, what he had with you was infinitely better.'

'You both knew, though, after the previous day, after that first kiss, after the second one anyway, you both knew what was going to happen.'

'Yes, I suppose so, and yet in spite of that . . .'

'Or because of that,' Kate said.

33

Bill brought home a girl. Her name was Joanna Parsons. They wanted to go up river in the *Argo*. Peter Workman came round; he and Bill finished painting the hull. When she was dry, two of the men came with a trailer and Bill and Peter helped them to launch her. The following morning they set off. Margaret had the children for the day; Peter made himself free to join them. Kate wore white jeans and her favourite Irish plaid shirt. 'Perfection,' Peter said.

Bill and Joanna sat in the bows, arms round their knees, intent over the green water. Peter watched Kate with vigilant admiration. His smile was a question masked as a response.

He said, 'It must be nice to have someone in the house.'

'Yes,' Kate said, 'yes, it is. At least it means one eats.'

'Haven't you been eating? You must eat.'

'It's no fun cooking when one's alone,' Kate said. 'On the other hand, of course, they don't exactly need my company.'

'She seems a very nice girl,' Peter said. 'Very pretty.'

'Do you think so?'

'They're not afraid to be attractive, these young girls nowadays, are they? They're not afraid of what they are, I mean. In our day, a sexy girl was always as jittery as a cook with a jelly in each hand.'

'What a funny idea!'

'Always afraid, always defensive, always thinking someone was going to slip something over on them when they weren't looking. They're not like that now. I suppose it's the pill. It's certainly something.'

'Did I tell you I had a burglar?' Kate said.

'No.'

'Well, I had a burglar.'

'When was this?'

'Last week.'

'Why didn't you say anything? What did he take?'

'Nothing. I got home before he'd finished.'

'You found him?'

'Yes,' Kate said. 'And off he went.'

'What did the police say?'

'It happens all the time,' Kate said.

'My God, I'll just bet you're glad to have Bill at home. You should have told me. I'd have come round. You shouldn't be in that house by yourself. It's dangerous.'

'I'm thinking of having a lodger,' Kate said. 'This looks nice, let's pull in here, we can picnic here.'

'What about swimming,' Bill said, 'can we or is it polluted?'

'It's all polluted,' Kate said, 'but probably a bit less up here. What do you think?'

'I'm a candidate,' Peter said.

'About the swimming.'

'It won't hurt,' Peter said, 'as long as you don't swallow more than a gallon or two. What sort of lodger?'

'A girl,' Kate said.

'Well, obviously,' Peter said. 'At least – '

'That way I shall be safe,' Kate said. 'Right? Even with a jelly in each hand.'

Bill and Joanna swam and were hungry. They lay under the willows, freckled by the drooping shade.

'They seem so serene,' Peter said. 'That's what gets me! Do you know, I hadn't only not kissed a girl at Bill's age, I was incapable of even talking to them?'

'They don't seem to need to talk.'

'It isn't only what they do,' Peter said. 'They seem so untroubled. He hasn't even got any spots. Spots and farting competitions, that's all I can remember. We had a perfectly dreadful attitude. Purity campaigns. Blackheads, smelly socks and purity campaigns. Pollution . . . I tell you.'

Kate said, 'You wore those dreadful socks. I can remember Richard had some. Great hairy things. No wonder your feet smelt.'

'Women are so beautiful,' Peter said, 'I still can't really believe they fancy us sometimes. What a day! What an absolutely marvellous day! Do you want another drop?' Peter had tilted the hock but Kate was on her feet and walking down towards the river. She squatted by the dusty water, the willows at her back, wedged into a segment of the bald bank. The tears ran down and starred the ground. It was like a nosebleed. She held her face over the earth so that nothing dropped on her shirt. The tears fell between her braced legs. She waited for them to stop.

Bill said, 'Listen, I think we might as well think about getting back, don't you?'

Joanna said, 'It's been superb. You're terrifically lucky having a boat and being on the river.'

Bill said, 'Kate . . . what do you think, go back?'

Kate said, 'Anything anyone likes.'

'I thought we could possibly press on up river a bit,

have tea somewhere,' Peter said. 'It's such a magnificent day.'

'Yes,' Kate said. 'Yes. Let's do that.'

'The boat's superb,' Bill said, 'only the thing is, I did tell someone it would be all right to telephone after about five.'

They went back. There were several boats moored at the anchorage above the weir. While Peter made the *Argo* fast, Bill and Joanna walked away towards the house.

Kate said, 'Bill, your sweater.'

Bill and Joanna had stopped to examine Joanna's foot. She seemed to have something in it. Bill said, 'Oh bring it, would you?'

Kate held the sweater out like a flag. Bill left Joanna holding her foot and ambled back.

'I also happen to have the picnic things to bring,' Kate said.

'I don't really need it,' Bill said.

'You'll get something in your foot if you go round like that.'

'I'm protected,' he said. 'I had my tetanus thing under a year ago.'

'You're not protected against a gash,' Kate said.

'All right,' Bill said, 'all right.'

Peter said, 'She's really nice. I'm glad we've got her back in the water.'

Kate said, 'Peter, will you do something? Will you sell her for me?'

'The old *Argo*?'

'I wish you would. I don't want her any more. Will you arrange it?'

34

Bill said, 'Rubbish. Junk. It's junk. People don't behave like that. He'd never do that. Would he, would
he ever do that?'

Joanna said, 'He might.'

'He never would. It's total junk.'

'I think I shall go to bed,' Kate said. 'Will you turn
it off when you've finished abusing the actors?'

'Sorry. Sorry. Were you taking it seriously?'

'No,' Kate said.

'It's not the actors,' Bill said. 'Not that I think
much of him. It's the script. It's what they're made to
do, what they're made to say.'

'What makes you an expert on what people do and
say?'

'Look, if you were listening seriously, I've already
apologized.'

'Oh I hate the damned thing,' Kate said.

'We obviously should have gone out,' Bill said.

'I was only wondering,' Kate said, 'how you managed to be so sure about how people behaved.'

'As if he'd do something like that right in the
middle of a dinner party. I mean, how much experience do you have to have to know a giraffe when you
see one?'

'A giraffe?'

'For the sake of example. A giraffe's a giraffe. Only
experienced people don't see giraffes when there are

giraffes to be seen. Experience is a way of not seeing things, if you ask me, not a way of seeing them. The older and wiser people get, the less they bother to notice and the more stupid they become.'

'Is he as aggressive as this at school?'

'He can be.'

'It's not aggression. Christ, it's not aggression. It was piss poor honestly, you must admit.'

'I thought it was dreadful,' Kate said. 'Does anyone want a hot drink or anything?'

'Not for me,' Joanna said.

'I think I'll have a beer. Have we got a beer? Jo?'

'Nothing for me,' Joanna said.

Kate said, 'I think I'll go on up. It doesn't mean you have to.'

'That's a relief,' Bill said. 'Oh God, there's a Part Three. I thought it was a bit inconclusive. Aren't you going to watch?'

'I think I've had enough,' Kate said.

'Oh stay and watch the last bit.'

Kate said, 'Will you switch things off?'

'The lot,' Bill said. 'Promise.'

'Goodnight, Joanna.'

'Goodnight.'

'Kate . . . ' He came out after her.

'What?'

'You're not upset, are you?'

'No. Not a bit.'

'A bit,' Bill said. 'You are a bit, aren't you? I'm sorry. I came on a bit strong. No offence.'

'That's all right,' Kate said.

'Do you like her?'

'She seems very nice. Not very talkative, but very nice.'

'She's quite bright actually. She's attractive, though, don't you think so?'

'Attractive,' Kate said, 'yes, I suppose she is. I suppose she must be. Nice teeth.'

'Nice teeth! You could tell when we were playing Scrabble', Bill said, 'how bright she was. "Narcosis" was a good shot, you must admit that.'

'You'd better go back,' Kate said, 'she'll think we're plotting something.'

'She doesn't think,' Bill said.

Kate said, 'Are you – ? It's none of my business, I'm sorry.'

'What? Oh come on.'

'Does she mean anything to you? Do you actually care about her? I mean . . .'

'Is it serious, you mean?'

'Well, yes, is it . . . ?'

'Guess,' Bill said.

35

She was doubtful about the fur cape, but in the end she packed it. She took the case out to the car where Bill and Joanna were waiting.

'Are you going somewhere, Kate?'

'Guess,' Kate said.

'With the suitcase, I meant. Where are you going?'

'I'm going to take you back to school,' Kate said.

'Aren't you cryptic, honestly! La Belle Dame Sans Merci! Sorry, I didn't mean to pry.'

They had to be back for first school on Monday morning. They arrived in front of the Centenary Buildings at the same time as a number of other punctual parents. Kate knew several of them; Bill had been at the school for five years. He would be relieved when she had gone; she would be relieved to have gone. The sight of the other parents did not sadden her; she was in no fear of weeping. They caused her a spasm of amused malice. She might have been part of some conspiracy to destroy the world on which their fortunes were founded. She treasured her secret like a weapon lying, oiled and deadly, in her suitcase.

'Well, listen, Kate, I'll give you a call,' Bill said. 'Maybe tomorrow. You will be there, won't you?'

'If I'm not,' Kate said, 'don't worry. It'll mean I'm out. I expect I shall.'

'You look a bit tricky,' Bill said. 'I don't know that I trust you. In the nicest possible way, of course. Seriously, I do expect you to be around. I shall take a dim view if you disappear. Mum.'

'I shan't disappear,' Kate said. 'You don't have to worry. I promise.'

He kissed her on both cheeks. 'I can always come up, no problem. If you want me, shout out, O.K.? Just don't . . . '

'I shall be fine. Goodbye, Joanna. Come again.'

'Thank you, I will.' She shook Kate's hand.

'You will, if you're asked,' Bill said. 'Come on, we'd better split or we shall get a whacking from Arrowsmith of the Remove.'

They ambled away, scuffing their wooden-heeled boots. The previous day they had been barefoot; now they were shod for the Russian winter. Kate shook her head and looked at her watch; an approaching parent stopped and waved, as if to cancel something. 'I can see you're in a hurry,' he said. 'I was only going to turn the screws on you over the Redevelopment Fund. Another time, another time.'

'If you don't mind,' Kate said.

'How's your husband, how's he keeping, is he all right?'

Kate said, 'You must excuse me, I ...'

'Give him my best. Pass him the word I shall be after him.'

Kate drove slowly. She looked often out of the side window. She could have been seeking a landmark or a difficult rendezvous. She turned off down a side road. There was a section of common, covered with gorse and bracken except where a flinty track went down towards a copse where the trees were so close and so thick that no grass grew between them. She parked the car and took the suitcase out of the boot. She walked down through the slippery wood and into the tall bracken. She came out at the top of a sloping meadow. Birds sang. She unsnapped the case and opened it. She selected two shirts, one blue, one white, a pair of grey trousers, green socks and a pair of brown shoes. She walked across the meadow to where molehills showed under the bramble hedge. She put down the clothes she had selected and spread them out. She carried handfuls of earth from a molehill and weighted down the open shirts and the trousers. She put stones or lumps of earth into the shoes and the socks.

When she had finished, she stood watching. Her mouth made little tasting motions. She frowned. She might have been a cook sipping a critical spoonful. She shrugged and turned and went up through the bracken. She stopped in the shoulder-high green and broke off the tip of a stalk. It was like a blind sea-horse curled on her hand. She took it to her lips and tasted its bitter bud. She spat it away and scrambled up through the trees towards the car. She was in sight of it when the bushes parted in front of her and a mounted man came cantering down the track towards her. He was followed by another figure, and another. A whole string of horses filled the track.

She stumbled back as they came streaming towards her. The drumming of their hooves was an assault. The riders came hacking past. Kate cowered from their beating charge. When they had gone, she ran gasping to the car. She had to stop in a layby and hold the wheel to control her shaking. She sat there for some minutes. She reasoned that the horsemen had turned away from the car. Probably they had not noticed it. Certainly they would not have troubled to take its number. She had nothing to fear.

There was a brown paper wastebag in a green metal container on the verge behind the layby. Kate went to the boot and, shielding the case from the pass-ing cars, took out the toaster. She held it in front of her as she took it to the wastebag. She had put on her gloves. She wiped the toaster with the rag from the car and then she dropped it into the bag. She threw the kitchen clock into a pond; Bill's transistor she wiped clean and then left in a supermarket trolley. She was tired when it came to the dinner jacket. It seemed like a piece of foreknowledge when she found the scarecrow. She went through the pockets for the furry vestiges of old cloakroom tickets and paper handkerchieves. She helped the scarecrow into the dinner jacket and buttoned the one button. She could not get him into the trousers. A broomstick gave him a third leg. She rolled the trousers into a neat cylinder and was bending to stuff them into a drain, when she saw that it was full of green slime. She walked on down the road. A new petrol station was being built. There were pumps under polythene hoods. Planks weighted more polythene over unset concrete. Kate saw a cavity under a section of dry concrete. She slotted the trousers into the darkness and told herself to walk slowly back to the car.

The dealer said, 'How much do you want for it?'

'Nothing,' Kate said. 'I just want to get rid of it.'

'Get rid of it? Is it yours?'

'Of course it's mine,' Kate said. 'What do you mean, is it mine? Would I be offering it to you if it wasn't?'

'May I ask your name?'

'No,' Kate said. 'I don't see that my name has anything to do with you.'

'You must forgive me,' the man said, 'but what made you come to me?'

'I was passing,' Kate said. 'Have you any objection? I've had rather a tiring day and I was passing and I thought I'd come in. You do advertise.'

'You'll forgive me,' the man said, 'but you're not in the trade, are you? I feel I've seen you.'

Kate said, 'I take it you don't want the silver.'

'I think you should go home. I have the feeling – and you'll forgive me for mentioning it – that you're not well maybe, that you're under some kind of a strain. Can I telephone somebody?'

'I'm perfectly well, I know what you're suggesting and I can promise you that I am not in the least unwell. I'm simply sick of silver. Is that inconceivable to you?'

'Madam – '

'I know you if it comes to that,' Kate said. 'And I don't accuse you of being mad.'

'I'm sorry. I was concerned, you excited my interest . . .'

'Perhaps you'd like to buy me,' Kate said.

'I have seen you,' the man said. 'And not so long ago.'

'You don't accept presents,' Kate said. 'Very well.'

'You see what it could lead to,' the man said.

'No, I don't. Explain.'

'How can I sell things people give me?' the man said. 'It's an impossibility. Can't you use ten pounds? Is this a question of principle? You're not giving me these things because you like me, let's be honest.'

'I have no further use for them,' Kate said. 'I thought you could dispose of them. I thought you would know where they could be disposed of. You know, in this country, getting rid of things poses a greater problem than you imagine. It is Mr Singer, isn't it?'

'Mr Singer, that's right, and you're – ?'

'I'm sorry if I came to the wrong man. I just happened to be passing and – '

'Try a charity,' the man said. 'If you really want to do some good, try a charity. They're always happy to have things.'

'I never said I wanted to do any good,' Kate said. 'What is good?'

36

The lights went out in the office. The last person was leaving. It was a man. He came out and locked the door behind him. The girl had not been at work. Kate had eaten nothing all day. Now she felt sick. The closed office was incredible to her. She flung open the door of the car, but she was not sick. When the man had gone, she ran across the street and the deep pavement and put her forehead to the smoked door. There was no one left. She watched herself in the mirroring surface, looking back at herself, a strange woman on the pavement. She ran to the car and drove to the girl's digs.

Josh said, 'Oh hi, hullo, how are you?'

Kate said, 'Is – is she here?'

Josh said, 'Who are you looking for?'

Kate said, 'You know, Miss – Miss – Miss Clavand. Miss Clavand.'

'Oh sure, of course, you're looking for Midge. I don't know. She could be. I didn't see her today.'

Kate pushed him aside and ran up the stairs. The door of the girl's room was not locked. She was in bed. She was ill. Kate said, 'Thank God.'

The girl said, 'My God, have I been sick.'

Kate said, 'This room! Who's been looking after you?'

The girl said, 'Looking after me? No one. No one. Who looks after anyone?'

'I could kick myself,' Kate said. 'I've wasted the whole day and I could have been here. I assumed you were working. I could have been here. How long have you been like this?'

'This is the third day,' the girl said. 'Since Friday.'

'You must have some air in here. You'll never get better. Have you actually been sick?'

'Have I? Dozens of times.'

'Why didn't you call me?'

'You had your son.'

'We spoke on Friday,' Kate said. 'You didn't say anything about not being well. You never said a word.'

'I was all right then. It started after.'

'You know what I'm going to do with you? I'm going to wrap you up in a blanket and take you home. You don't think you can stay here like this, do you? When were you last sick?'

'I don't know exactly. Time is very strange. Maybe an hour, maybe more, maybe less.'

'Have you got a suitcase?'

'No, not really,' the girl said. 'There's a sack somewhere. You know my sack. Darling, there's really no need, you know. I'm getting better now.'

'There's every need,' Kate said. 'I've got an empty suitcase in the car. Does your office know you're ill?'

'Oh my office!' the girl said.

'It's not healthy,' Kate said, 'that office. It's dark and it's gloomy. It's not healthy. Lights on all day. And this place – well, it isn't exactly sanitary, is it? How does that man always manage to be cooking curry every time I come here?'

'Noonie? He's lovely, he's nice. He's an addict. It really is a horrible odour, isn't it?'

'Come on,' Kate said, 'we're getting you out of this. I'll go and get the case.'

She took Mijo home and put her to bed in the spare room. In clean sheets, in the small, bright room, she looked frail and grateful. She reached for Kate's hand.

'Darling, thank you.'

'That place was absurd,' Kate said. 'I should never have let you stay there. And I have no doubt you were being robbed. I wish I'd known earlier, that's all, about . . . Never mind, you're here now, where I can look after you properly. You'll soon be better.'

'I'm better now,' the girl said.

Two days later, Mijo was sitting in a deck chair in the garden. She was still pale and weak.

'I'm very pleased with you,' Kate said. 'All that I ask now is that you don't rush things. Could you eat an omelette, do you think, for lunch? I promise not to overcook it!'

'Let me do it,' the girl said.

Kate pressed her into the deck chair and went down the steps to the kitchen. The girl turned her face to the sun and closed her eyes. Kate put the butter into the pan and went to whisk the eggs. The telephone rang in the hall.

'Kate?'

'Oh hullo, Mummy, how are you?'

'I'm all right,' Mrs Sells said, 'but how are you?'

'As a matter of fact I'm exceptionally well, why?'

'Are you? Are you really? I wanted to call you yesterday, but I was up to my ears. You know, I was thinking: we ought to do a theatre. There're heaps of good things on in the West End at the moment. Or a concert. You really are all right, though, are you? Because do say.'

'Yes,' Kate said, 'I – '

'You're not worried about money for instance?'

'Money?'

'Everything's working out all right? They're not keeping you short? I remember when your father died, there was a terrible gap – '

'No, the bank's been fine, and so's David Bogen, our solicitor; it's all been very – what? – sensibly worked out. Why do you ask?'

'I hope you've been seeing enough people,' Mrs Sells said. 'You haven't been brooding on your own too much?'

'I'm fine,' Kate said.

Mrs Sells said, 'I was wondering if you'd like to come to a sale next week. There's one on down near Crawley, that wouldn't be too far for you.'

'No, Mummy, thank you. I've got plenty to do.'

'If you need money or have any problems of that nature, you will let me know, won't you?'

Kate said, 'My God, Mummy, I must run. I'll call you later.'

The stove was in flames.

Kate said, 'Mijo! Mijo!'

The girl looked round the striped chair. Kate turned out the gas, but flames were leaping up the wall. The girl ran down into the kitchen, snatched the black handle of the omelette pan and flung it through the open door on to the paved terrace. It flamed for a few seconds and then died.

Kate said, 'Didn't you see it? Didn't you see what was happening?'

'I'm sorry, darling. I was facing the other direction and –'

'Your friend Noonie's curry has obviously spoiled your sense of smell. Have you burnt yourself? It was Noonie, wasn't it?'

'Noonie, yes. It's nothing. It's nothing at all. Just a bit red –'

'Under the cold tap,' Kate said, 'go on. We might have burnt the house down. We were lucky, I suppose. It's only scorched, it ought to wash off. Mrs Jenkins can do it in the morning.'

'No, we'll do it,' the girl said.

'How is it, the hand, all right? You're not going to do anything whatsoever. I want you to get your strength back.'

'You're right. I should have seen what was happening,' the girl said. 'I'm sorry.'

'My silly mother,' Kate said, 'I still don't know what she wanted. Oh God, not again!'

'You answer,' the girl said, 'and I'll do the omelette.'

'There's another pan under the sink. The eggs are all mixed. Hullo.'

'Kate?'

'Mummy –'

'What happened? You suddenly –'

'A minor drama in the kitchen. Nothing at all. I said I'd call you back.'

'You sounded –'

'I told you, I'm fine, I'm absolutely fine. Is something wrong with you?'

'Not in the least,' Mrs Sells said. 'I was just hoping we could meet.'

Kate said, 'Yes, you said. Maybe we can do a theatre – '

'I've got some news as a matter of fact, that I wanted to tell you. I'm going in with Petie.'

'Petie,' Kate said.

'Petie Foreshaw. The Colonel. He's asked me to go in with him and I've decided I will. Basically he wants to buy me out, but I can't go on handling heavy pieces by myself indefinitely, and Lionel's been away more and more often with his daughter.'

'What will you do about Stiles?'

'Oh Stiles, I shall keep Stiles, certainly for the moment, at least until we see how things work out.'

'I hope he's going to pay you well,' Kate said.

'He's going to look after me very nicely,' Mrs Sells said, 'don't you worry.'

Kate said, 'Well, congratulations.'

'I shall be very well looked after. So if you need anything, remember . . . '

'Mummy, I must go.'

'Kate, just one thing. You haven't by any chance bumped into my friend Wolf Singer, have you, on your travels lately?'

'Travels? What travels?'

'Only he called me the other day about something else and I got the impression, probably wrongly, that you might have bumped into him.'

'My goodness me, what sharp eyes you've all got. One can't get away with anything with you around.'

'What do you mean, get away with anything?'

'I haven't bumped into anybody,' Kate said.

The omelette was waiting.

Kate said, 'And I wanted to do it for you.'

'Oh boff! It's time I did something. I'm all right now.

'I don't want you going back to work too soon,' Kate said. 'You know, I've been thinking, only I wasn't going to mention it yet, we really ought to take you away somewhere and help you recuperate.'

'Oh la,' the girl said, 'I haven't got a consumption or anything like that. My stomach was upset.'

'I don't want to stay here,' Kate said.

'Such a beautiful house,' the girl said.

'You said you wanted to go to Mexico,' Kate said.

'One day, one day, but not to recover from a stomach. Besides, they are famous for stomachs. Montezuma's Revenge, surely you've heard of that?'

Kate said, 'All I mean is, we ought to do things. I mean, what particular virtue is there in working in some dingy office? Is that really what you want to do? And England – '

'Darling, I can't just – '

'I don't want to spend the rest of my days looking after this house. I want to do things. What do you mean Montezuma's Revenge?'

'It's the stomach trouble people get in Mexico. They call it – '

'Oh yes, of course, I saw something about it. What's to stop us just packing up when we want to and going? I can't think of anything.'

The girl said: 'Darling, if you give me a cloth, I'm going to make a start on this wall of yours. It worries me.'

'I wouldn't mind if the whole house had burned down,' Kate said.

'Kate,' the girl said, 'darling! Why? It's so nice. I'm so happy just now, aren't you? Aren't you? Just the two of us.'

37

The girl said, 'Darling, I must go sometime, if only to tell them what's happened.'

'I'll go,' Kate said, 'if you want me to. Gladly.'

'No, no. I'm all right now. I slept so well. I feel wonderful this morning. Truly. I feel perfectly fine now. I can go. I want to go.'

'How much do you pay for that room?' Kate said.

'How much do I pay? I pay nine pounds fifty a week. It's more than a room. It's two rooms.'

'You're being robbed, I presume you know that? You can have this room for nothing. You can live here for nothing. You've got the bathroom. It's not as though you can't do whatever you like. You can come and go just as you please. That way you can save, save for what you want to do.'

'Oh darling,' the girl said, 'how practical you are! And how unromantic! As if the only reason I would want to stay here is because of the plumbing! Darling, really, you are funny.'

'Then what shall we do?' Kate said. 'Shall we go and get your things? Shouldn't you give notice, I mean, and clear your stuff? And what about the job?'

'I'll go and see them,' the girl said. 'I'll go and have a talk with them.'

'I'll take you in the car,' Kate said. 'And afterwards we can get your things.'

'Kate, darling . . . ' She put her arms round Kate's

neck and stared into her eyes. 'You are going to promise me something now. You must. You will not try to do everything for me. You will not spoil me. You must promise me because otherwise ... Otherwise I turn into a completely lazy person. Believe me, it can happen very quickly with me. You know I am half vegetable. I must work, because if I don't work, I shall do nothing. One day maybe we go on our trip and then I stop, but until then ... So, you promise?'

'I don't even know what I'm promising,' Kate said.

'But you do promise?'

'If we go in the car,' Kate said, 'we can put all your things in it, it will be so easy, all in one go.'

'I'll be back,' the girl said, 'I promise you. I'm not a baby, you know. Not yet. Kiss me, darling. Kiss me. Kiss me here. Come.'

Kate said, 'Mrs Jenkins ... '

The girl said, 'Shut the door, my darling. She hasn't even arrived.'

'That's the thing, as soon as she does, she always wants to see me. She's always got something she wants to tell me. Tonight.'

'You go downstairs, darling, you are quite right. Then you can be there when Mrs Jenkins arrives. You go down.'

Kate made tea and some toast and put the muesli on the table. Mijo was a long time, but Kate could not begin without her. She sat with the paper. When she came down, the girl was dressed in her jeans and her yellow P.V.C. top.

Kate said, 'You were quick. When will you be back?'

'Oh, this afternoon, sometime. Not late.'

'Do you want an egg?'

150

'Oh no really, I must run.' She put butter and marmalade on her toast. 'I'll get some coffee later.'

Kate said, 'A minute ago – '

The girl said, 'Was a minute ago. Now if I hurry I can get everything done and then tonight . . . '

Mrs Jenkins's key sounded in the front door. The girl jumped up and kissed Kate and ran out of the kitchen. While Mrs Jenkins told Kate how over eighty pounds' worth of damage had been done to her husband's car when it was stationary at the lights, Kate ate the crusts which Mijo had left on her plate. She fitted her teeth into the crescents left by the girl. And then it turned out the man was not even insured.

38

'So you're not leaving,' Kate said.

'Not for the moment,' the girl said.

'You're going to carry on.'

'They asked me. You know, they were a bit – '

'You're too easily swayed,' Kate said.

'Oh la, it's not a terrible thing. I have to make some money. If it's not that job, it's another one. I can't just sit here all day, can I?'

'You're too intelligent to be a dogsbody,' Kate said, 'but it's your business. You should look for something more demanding.'

'I've got you,' the girl said.

'That's nasty. I'm not demanding. I certainly don't mean to be. If ever I am, then I want you to promise to say so. Promise. If I ever try to make you do things you don't want to do, if I ever try to interfere with you – well, with your private affairs, if I make demands, I want you to tell me off. Seriously. Promise you will?'

'If you insist,' the girl said.

'You were a long time telling them you'd carry on. Did you stop and do some work?'

'I had some things to do. For instance, I went to an agency about other jobs. Something more demanding perhaps.'

Kate said, 'Anyway for the moment you're settled.'

That evening, the girl had a telephone call. It was the first time anyone had asked for her. Kate did not recognize the voice, but she recognized the girl's chuckle as she spoke to whoever it was. When she came back into the room, the girl sat down and resumed her book.

Kate said, 'Is everything all right?'

'Yes, darling, of course. Perfectly all right. Darling, will it be all right if I'm not in tomorrow night?'

'Of course,' Kate said. 'Of course.'

'You are sweet to me, darling.'

Kate said, 'You're free to come and go exactly as you like, you know that.'

'I don't really want to go, but I have to. It's family, my cousin.'

'You should go to bed,' Kate said. 'You look tired. You're still not really recovered.'

'I'm perfectly well; a little tired, yes, but that's all. I read in bed.'

'That's right. You go to bed and I'll bring you a drink.'

'Darling, you've done enough,' the girl said, 'too much.' She came back and kissed Kate on each cheek. 'Good night.'

While Kate was locking up, Peter Workman telephoned. She agreed to see him the following evening. As soon as she had put down the telephone, she went round the house and made sure that every door was locked and every window secure before she went upstairs. She knocked and went into the girl's room. The light was not out. She said, 'In case I forget in the morning, I want to give you a key. You mustn't depend on me being in all the time.'

The girl said, 'Oh yes, darling, thank you. I won't be late though, if you're thinking of tomorrow.'

'I'm not only thinking of tomorrow,' Kate said. She bent and kissed Mijo on each cheek. 'Now you get a good night's sleep. I want you well.'

'Darling – '

'Yes?'

'Perhaps we go out to a theatre next week.'

'We'll see,' Kate said, 'we'll see.'

'Are you going to bed now?'

'Yes,' Kate said. 'I'm going to have a bath and then I shall.'

'Shall I come in?'

'If you want to,' Kate said. 'Are you sure you're all right?'

'You're not angry with me?'

'Angry?' Kate said. 'Me? Do I look angry?'

'No,' the girl said.

39

Peter Workman suggested they go to the same restaurant. 'Admittedly it wasn't all that special when
we went, but I've heard tremendous reports since
from other people. Probably we just struck a bad
night.'

Kate said, 'What an optimist you are!'

'Well, I liked the atmosphere. It's the sort of place
where you can talk.'

'We can talk at home,' Kate said.

'Ah but whose home,' Peter said. 'That's the problem. Circumstances alter cases. I gather you've got
your lodger all arranged.'

'Yes,' Kate said. 'How did you gather that?'

'Somebody saw something, you know how it is.'

'It's the girl who used to work in the office, actually,' Kate said. 'The girl who worked with Richard.
She came round because he'd lent her some books.
Also I think she wanted to offer her, you know, her
condolences and we started to talk. She seems a very
nice sort of girl. And of course she was very fond of
Richard which gives us something in common, I suppose. We lead entirely separate lives obviously.'

Peter said, 'Yes, I was sorry she went. I think
Richard's death really shook her. Of course it's different living in the house, I suppose, from carrying on at
the office.'

Kate said, 'I had the room and she was looking for

somewhere. I'm cadging French lessons, but otherwise it's a strictly business arrangement.'

'It gives you somebody in the house at least,' Peter said. 'These menus get coyer and coyer, don't they? I mean, Sweets for the Sweet, that's rather overdoing things, don't you think, in the humour department?'

'Oh Peter,' Kate said, 'I never thought to hear you criticize anyone for that.'

'You know, Kate, I don't actually think of life as at all funny. I mean, I'm not amused personally. I'm actually rather a glum soul. I'm usually covering up.'

Kate said, 'Oh I think that's true of most of us.'

'I suppose glumness isn't much of a recommendation for oneself. I'm not sure I even mean glum; I think perhaps I mean just plain serious. I've been listening to a lot of music since I've been on my own. I'm very keen on these stereo headphones. You seem to be able to take right off from the world. You're absolutely surrounded with sound, have you tried them at all?'

'I keep meaning to,' Kate said.

'Because you have this sensation of being alone in a great world full of sound and yet no one else can hear a thing. The sound's completely unpolluted, that's what I find. Nothing between you and it. Perfect marriage sort of business. You must try it. Now look, we'd better order and then we can get back to the higher musicology.'

They were tempted by one or two exotic things they had never tried. Peter thought the way they did brains sounded rather terrific; Kate agreed, but in the end they had the same meal they had had the previous time. It tasted much better. What had been tough was now tender; the tepid was hot, the sauce smooth. When the meal was over, the waiter came promptly with second cups of coffee.

Peter said, 'How's the wound, Kate?'

'How's the wound? It's there. It's there.'

'And I don't suppose you really want it not to be.'

'One hates the pain, one dreads the healing.'

'Will it distress you if I say how beautiful you look?'

'Probably the wine,' Kate said.

'Oh I don't flatter myself it's me,' Peter said.

'And being with you. Being with someone one knows and has known for a long time.'

'What about some brandy?' Peter said. 'Or a crème de menthe frappé. They look rather choice.'

'No, I really don't want anything else.'

'I hope we shall always know each other,' Peter said.

'You know how much I rely on you. Probably too much.'

'You can never ask too much of me,' Peter said. 'I'll get the bill and we can be on our way.'

In the car, she said, 'Who've you got babysitting?'

'Oh,' he said, 'the girl. Helga. She's got a bit of a cold actually, she's probably in bed, but it's at least somebody to see they don't get burnt to a crisp. Do you feel like coming in for a bit? Or what? I was sort of assuming you'd be wanting to buzz off home, I don't know why.'

'The lodger's got a key,' Kate said.

'You know I love you, don't you? You know I love you very much indeed.'

Kate said, 'Dear Peter.'

'Because I do,' he said, 'and nothing to do with anything.'

She turned and leaned forward and kissed him on the lips. She put her arms round his neck and kissed him on the lips and watched his face as it flared in the light of a passing car.

'Come in,' he said. 'Everyone's asleep. Come in.'

'For a minute,' she said.

'I can probably manage to find a drop of something.'

He was busy on his errand for a bottle and glasses. When he came into the drawing-room, she took them from him and put them on the Welsh dresser.

He said, 'Kate, are you being kind?'

She said, 'Is it forbidden?'

'You don't have to be kind to me,' he said.

'You have to to me,' she said.

'Oh Kate,' he said, 'I don't know.'

She said, 'Is there a lock? I'm sorry, but –'

Peter said, 'Come upstairs.'

'No,' she said. 'I don't want to do that. Put something in front of the door.' He began to move furniture. 'Not everything, just something.' He was busy while she unzipped her dress. He turned out the main light. She said, 'Peter?'

'I didn't plan this, you know,' he said.

'No?' she said. 'I did.'

'Look – forgive me, but –'

'It's all right,' Kate said.

'At our age!' Peter said.

'We're not past it yet,' Kate said. 'Quite, are we?'

'I love you. I love you. I've been so damned unhappy. You're the only thing I've thought about all these weeks.'

'That's all right,' Kate said. 'That's all right, don't, don't.'

'Blubbing like a kid,' Peter said. 'Christ Almighty, I'm so happy. I said you were beautiful and you are beautiful, more beautiful than I even imagined, and I did imagine.'

Kate said, 'Not as beautiful as I was.'

'I saw you once before. You aren't any less beautiful now.'

'When? When did you?'

'When we took that place together, down in Bandol that time. Very nearly the end of friendship, partnership and everything elseship, if you remember.'

'Oh God, that terrible so-called villa. The Maison what was it? The Maison Calanque. How much one forgets. You saw me without my clothes on?'

'Afraid I did, yes. Through the window. You were washing your hair under the shower. You were wearing a sort of turban of suds, I remember, and nothing else. I've never forgotten. You had the windows open and ... well, there we were. You never knew?'

'I suppose I must have left the window open for some reason,' Kate said. 'Though it isn't honestly the sort of thing I usually do.'

'I was going to say,' Peter said.

Kate said, 'It's all right, it's all right.'

Peter said, 'But you, what about you?'

'Please,' she said, 'don't – don't think about me.'

'Oh Kate,' he said, 'oh Kate, oh Kate, oh darling.'

'Yes,' she said, 'Peter. Yes, my love.'

40

Kate did nothing to stop the sobs. She sat and listened to them. From time to time she moved her head or re-arranged herself in the chintz chair under the red oar.

'He hates me,' Margaret said. 'He hates me.'

Kate said, 'You still haven't told me what actually happened.'

'He must. He must. To do something like he did. It's the most horrible thing that ever happened to me in my whole life. He must hate me. It's the only ex-planation that makes any sort of sense. And he wanted me to come and live with him. He begged me to. He cried. He actually cried.'

'When was this?'

'Oh before – before –' Margaret was working to get a hair out of her mouth. 'Before I went to live with him finally. When I was still at home. I hate him. I hate him. I'd like to kill him. I really mean it. I'd like to kill him. I've never felt like this before in my life.'

Kate said, 'When did all this blow up?'

'Bastard. Bloody swine. He's a bloody swine. Of course he's a big baby. He's nothing but a big baby. He doesn't know what he really wants in any way, shape or form. He's as good as admitted that several times in the last few weeks.'

'I thought you were going to get married.'

'He could never be married to anybody. He doesn't know what marriage is. He doesn't know what it is to care for anybody. How could I ever have been such a fool?'

'I don't think you've been a fool,' Kate said.

'I've been an utter fool. The thing is, he acts surprised. Do you know what he did? Kate, do you know what he did? He only tried to pass me on to somebody else, that's all. I was at the flat and this man came, this American, a man he'd met in Los Angeles, and it was obvious. He as good as told me that David had said . . . '

'What man?'

'An American, an executive from one of these companies they sell things to or buy things from; he just turned up and said that David had said the apartment was his whenever he wanted it and everything that went with it.'

'Oh but that's not necessarily evidence of anything!'

'David's in a club. He's in a club.'

'Oh come on, Mag, I don't believe it. I just don't believe it.'

'You've been seeing Peter,' Margaret said. 'David's in a club, I tell you. They're all the same. The Studs. Can you believe it? I couldn't believe it. Studs!'

'How do you know David had anything to do with this man? He was probably just in town and thought . . . '

'I called David, that's how. I thought the same as you, and I called David, I was so angry, I was so – He was in Munich for some European telecommunications conference. I called him and I just couldn't believe my ears. Do you know what he said? He said, "It won't do you any harm to be nice to a visiting fireman," that's what he said.'

'A visiting fireman.'

'I said, "You've got to be joking," and he just said, "Phil's an old mate." He doesn't love me, Kate, that's the thing. He doesn't mean the same thing I mean by anything.'

'Did you see him when he came back?'

'I saw him,' Margaret said. 'I was sure it was all a misunderstanding. Well, it wasn't. It just wasn't. Good God, wanting me to go to bed with someone I'd never even met, someone . . . He treated me like – like a spare bed. Like a spare bed, Kate. Like a nothing person. An absolute nothing person. I tried to laugh it all off. I tried to make a joke of it. And do you know what he said eventually? He'd been drinking on the plane. He said, "Oh Christ, woman, what's one fuck more or less between friends?" I'm sorry, but those were his actual words.'

'You're hysterical,' Kate said.

'I suppose he'd been shagging some teenage prostitute in Munich. Some blonde teenager with big titties. They all do it. Nothing means anything to them any more, any of them. I hate them. I hate them all. I wish I didn't have to have anything further to do with them. Trying to pass me on to a – a man of fifty-five with a paunch. How could he? I could kill him, I really mean it, Kate. And now what am I going to do?'

'Why don't you go and see Peter?'

'Oh he's always such a clown. He never knows what to say about anything.'

'I don't find him like that.'

'I don't want to see anybody.'

'I wondered what brought you here.'

'Oh Kate, don't. You know I don't mean that.

161

You're always so sane. It's such a pleasure to talk to someone who's got a sensible outlook. Someone balanced. I know I'm being selfish and awful, so don't bother to tell me, using you like Kleenex, because I know very well.'

Kate said, 'Have you told him you're leaving?'

'I've left. I haven't told him anything. I don't need to. I've simply packed up and left. What's still there can stay there. I shan't ever go back. He just expected me to go to bed with him, this man, Phil Bean. Phil Bean! Apparently I was supposed to take off my clothes and get straight into bed with him. Do you know he actually said I was disloyal? Disloyal! He actually said that. Goodbye! I haven't got a job either, come to that. I shall put in for a transfer and see what happens. He's got so much swing, David, he'll probably have me out on my ear. I'm only a temporary contract. He's such a viciously vindictive little bastard when he wants to be. I've seen him. You know he's only five feet five inches tall? That's probably what accounts for this tremendous drive he's got, and of course he's got to prove himself with every woman under sixty he ever comes across. I don't even know where I'm going to sleep.'

'You ought to go home to Peter,' Kate said, 'it's the obvious thing.'

'Oh and then I shall have the children all over me demanding explanations. I tell you, Kate, I'm just about all in, I'm bushed, I really am. Another set of inquiring faces and I shall go spare, I know I shall. I'm a selfish bitch.'

'When did you last eat?' Kate said. 'Suppose I make you some food?'

162

'I couldn't. I'm sorry. Forgive me. I'll try and pull myself together. How are you? You look marvellous, considering. What a lovely cameo that is! I don't think I've ever seen it before.'

'I've had it ages,' Kate said. 'I think you should see Peter. Richard gave it to me.'

'You know, you're the only person I can really talk to when I feel like this, I don't know why.'

Kate said, 'Why do people like that always have to talk about marriage? No one has to talk about marriage if they don't want to.'

'The more insincere people are, the more they talk about sincerity. They want to be sincere, but they can't. And people who are really frightened of marriage, who don't really think they can ever make a success of it, they always have to talk about it for the same reason –'

Kate said, 'Put it down to experience.'

'That's the only thing to do, I suppose, you're quite right. You know what he said to me quite seriously? He told me Deirdre was the only woman who had ever understood him properly. Deirdre! He hates her.'

Kate said, 'Put it behind you. You made a mistake. Put it behind you.'

Margaret said, 'Kate, shall I tell you something awful? I am angry, I do hate him, but in the last day or two I keep thinking "I wish I had gone to bed with the man." What would it have mattered? Suppose I'd let him have his randy ram, what would it really have mattered? You know the truth? I wish to God I had gone to bed with him.'

41

The girl had not come home. When the telephone rang, it was Peter Workman.

'Kate? How are you?'

'I'm all right. I'm fine.'

'Kate, I've got Mag here.'

'She said she wanted to come back, but she was afraid. I told her she should, I hope I did right.'

'God knows what he's done to her. She's asleep at the moment, I think, but she's been through absolute hell. What did you make of her?'

Kate was sitting in the unlit hall, on the bottom step of the stairs. She said, 'She let herself in for more than she bargained for.'

'That's what she bargained for,' Peter said. 'Only she didn't know just how much more. He seems to have been a right bastard. But then, as I say, that presumably was the idea.'

'It made a change,' Kate said.

'Sorry?'

'No one could accuse you of being a bastard.'

'I was hoping to see you,' Peter said, 'as per plan. But I suppose we shall really have to put the stoppers on that for the moment.'

'It doesn't matter,' Kate said.

'It matters like hell to me, my love. The thing being, though, I did make her promise that if she ever wanted to she'd come back – And now she's here, well, you can guess how it is.'

'She must be very grateful,' Kate said. 'I know she is actually. She realizes what a ghastly mistake she made. She loves you very much.'

'Which more or less puts the ki-bosh on us for the time being. I just don't think I can break it to Mag at the present.'

Kate said, 'Of course you can't. You can't possibly.'

'God, you're understanding,' Peter said. 'You're the most amazing, understanding woman I ever knew in all my life. I hope I haven't hurt you. I hope it doesn't mean I've hurt you.'

'I shall survive,' Kate said.

'Kate?'

'I'm still here,' Kate said.

'This doesn't negate anything I said to you. I still feel exactly as I did last night. More so, if anything. I don't know about you.'

'I still feel the same too,' Kate said. 'Give my love to Margaret. And the children.'

Peter said, 'Kate, I shall always be here. Always.'

'I know,' Kate said.

She went upstairs, without turning on a light, and into the girl's room. It was no longer as tidy as it had been the first day or two. One of the drawers in the little chest was half open. A blouse lolled out of it. The orange sleeve caught the last of the light through the uncurtained window. A false dawn seemed to come from the reflection of the setting sun, which was already below the horizon.

Kate sat on the narrow bed. Then she stretched out, with her hands behind her neck, and watched the pearly light fade on the ceiling. From the towpath came the last shouts of the day. A practice crew, from one of the clubs belonging to a business house, was being coached through a megaphone.

She went and drew the curtains and then turned on the light. It seemed to waken the girl's things. Kate began to search. When she had looked, she put everything back in its exact place: one of them in the wrong place and the girl would know. The lolling sleeve was like a shamming sleeper. The wrist fell back. In the half-drawer at the top of the dresser were make-up pots and eye-pencils; and a card of pills. Half the course had gone. The girl was still taking them. Kate checked that the room was as it had been and turned out the light. She went downstairs. It was night. She went and sat in the dark drawing-room, under the oar, and waited.

When she heard the girl opening the front gate, she got up and went through into the kitchen. She looked out of the window on to the garden. She opened the back door and went out. Someone was there. She returned to the kitchen and felt in the drawer for the meat cleaver. Then she went back into the garden. She climbed the steps to the lawn and walked towards where the hammock faced the river. She made no attempt to conceal herself. The couple were lying on the far side of the hammock, under the big lilac from which she had been cutting brown flowers.

Kate said, 'How dare you use my hammock cushions?'

She was too late to stop them. They moved together to a dumb climax under her eyes; she had never seen such a thing before. She watched them like a nurse.

She said, 'Unless you go at once, I shall call the police.' She spoke in a soft voice. In the house, a light went on. Its faint yellow came across the lawn towards them.

The girl sat up and said, 'I told you we shouldn't, stupid.'

Kate said, 'Will you please go and not come back?'

The couple limped towards the gate. The young man came back, doing his belt up. 'I'll put the cushion back for you.'

'Just go,' Kate said, 'thank you very much.'

It was not the first time there had been a couple in the garden. They came along the towpath from the Bunch of Grapes. Richard used to find contraceptives in the watering can. Once he sat up with an air-gun.

The girl was calling for Kate in the house. Kate stayed outside the back door until she went upstairs. A square of light fell on her like a cat from the landing window. She heard the bath running. Then she went in. She still carried the cleaver. Her bedroom door was now ajar. The girl must have looked in. Kate stood behind the door while the girl went from her bedroom to the bathroom. She saw her pale body go past, through the crack in the door. Kate slipped off her shoes. The girl went into the bathroom. Kate padded across the landing to the creaking board and pressed her weight on to it. The board creaked. There was silence from the bathroom. Kate leaned once more on the board. The creak was louder.

The girl said, 'Who's there? Kate, is that you? Darling?'

Kate allowed the board one more faint creak and then crossed the landing to the stairs and went down.

The girl said, 'Kate?' Her voice came from the landing. 'Who's there?'

Kate stood behind the drawing-room door.

The girl said, 'Come on, don't be a fool, is there anyone there? Kate, darling, is that you?' She was coming down the stairs. Kate ran across the sitting-room and lay down behind the Chesterfield. The light went on in the hall. The girl was in the kitchen. Kate had left the door open. The girl called into the garden. 'Kate? Who is that? Get away or I call the police. Go away.'

She came back and shut the door. The drawer was open. She pushed it shut. Kate heard the bang. She had opened one of the drawing-room windows and was over the sill by the time the girl came into the room. She crouched against the bricks. She heard the girl in the room and scampered round to the shelter of the front porch before Mijo came to the open window and leaned out. She shut the window and ran into the hall. Kate heard the ting of the phone being picked up. She hesitated and then ran down the path at the side of the house. A few seconds later, she was at the back door. She tapped with her nails. The light was on. The girl had turned on every light in the house. Her face was white as she came to the door.

'Mijo, what's happened?'

'There was a man here,' the girl said. 'I called the police.'

'There was someone in the garden,' Kate said. 'I went to see. It wasn't you, was it?'

'There's been someone in the house,' the girl said. 'I was having a bath.'

'Are you sure?'

'Where were you? I know there was someone. Oh darling! I'm so glad to see you.'

'You poor girl, you poor sweet. How long have you been home? I saw the light go on, I was down on the towpath, I was afraid perhaps it was someone who shouldn't be there. I was frightened myself. You were so late.'

'I've been home a few minutes, long enough to get in the bath. That must be the police.'

'What shall we say?'

'Darling, I was frightened. I was really frightened, I don't mind telling you. I really didn't know what was going to happen.'

'No,' Kate said, 'nor did I.'

She put the cleaver back in the drawer and went to meet the police.

42

'Do they always ask so many questions, your police? I thought they were going to stay all night.'

'If you call them,' Kate said.

'They seemed to suspect us,' the girl said.

'I suppose some people try and make fools of them.'

'I did see a shadow,' the girl said, 'or I thought I did.'

'You can't identify a shadow,' Kate said. 'Can you?'

'And then, of course, in the middle I realized I had only my robe on and nothing else. What do you think they thought?'

'I don't think they thought anything. Oh maybe with one side of their heads, I don't know. But all they care about is whether there's going to be someone to charge with something. I'm sorry you were frightened.'

'God,' the girl said, 'my bath! It'll be freezing.'

'You should never get out of a bath,' Kate said. 'I'm sure no one would ever attack you if you were lying in a bath.'

'No? I was angry,' the girl said. 'Someone coming into this house! I was angry. I think they might.'

Kate said, 'There was a man, I was forgetting, who murdered his brides in their baths. Quite painless. But that was a long time ago. Are you really going to get back in or – ?'

The girl said, 'I'd better pull the curtains.'

'Oh the curtains! Damn the curtains! He used to pull them under by the feet and there was nothing they could do. Did you have a nice evening?'

'I was with some people, it wasn't bad. We went to a few places.'

'Friends?' Kate said. 'Once their heads were under.'

'Yes, friends. Well, some friends . . .'

'You have nice feet. Very nice. You were quite a group, were you?'

The girl said, 'Oh darling, don't darling, don't, not here.'

'Including that American?'

'American? I'm getting out. Be careful.'

'Including Josh? We should powder you,' Kate said. 'We should put some powder on you.'

'They were some friends,' the girl said. 'Mostly French. People who are over here. No one to be jealous about.'

'I'm not jealous,' Kate said. 'I have no right to be jealous. I'll tell you what. I've got some lovely powder. I'll give you some of that. Some powder Richard gave me. Did he ever give you any powder?'

'No,' said the girl. 'Darling, are you all right tonight? What have you been doing? Have you been by yourself?'

'You like him, don't you? That American. The one I met.'

'Not particularly.'

'I'm not jealous,' Kate said.

'I don't like him particularly. Sometimes he's all right. Why do you ask about him particularly?'

'Oh no reason,' Kate said. 'My room or your room? My room, don't you think so?'

'I'll do the curtains,' the girl said.

'No,' Kate said, 'I'll do everything. I'll do everything. Just leave everything to me.'

'I think I'm a little frightened of you tonight, darling,' the girl said. 'You're being so kind to me.'

'This is the powder.'

'As if you had intentions,' the girl said. 'Are we leaving the light?'

'I could look at you for ever,' Kate said. 'I'd like to be here with you for ever. I'd like to give you everything you want, everything. I'd like to love every inch of you. Every centimetre.'

The girl said, 'Why aren't you coming? Please come to bed properly.'

'Because I want you to realize, my little Mijo, I want you to realize that I don't want anything from you. I don't want you to do anything for me at all. Nothing.'

'Oh darling, no, please.'

'I want you to know how much I want to do for you. And I don't want you to do anything at all. Not a thing.'

'Oh darling, no.'

'Give me at least that pleasure, my little one,' Kate said.

43

Kate said, 'Tell me something else about Richard.'

'What can I tell you that you don't know?'

'Oh a lot, I dare say,' Kate said. 'Everything. Did he amuse you? Did you laugh?'

'Not so much,' the girl said. 'I don't think we laughed so much. Did you?'

'They all made a lot of jokes,' Kate said. 'That generation.'

'You were too nice to me,' the girl said. 'I don't think that should happen, you being as nice as that, it's not what I like.'

'I wanted you to see how much I care about you.'

'What exactly do you mean about that generation?' the girl said. 'You think Richard wasn't serious?'

'He was worried when you weren't smiling, when you weren't amused. He thought it was his duty to keep you smiling. He wasn't like that with you?'

'He was rather serious, I think, a bit of a mystic even. Especially about gardens. He liked to give people exactly what they wanted, what they needed, for him it was a kind of psychological thing, to guess. He was almost feminine like that.'

'Feminine!'

'He had intuitions,' the girl said. 'Don't you talk about intuition?'

'It wasn't that,' Kate said. 'It was the idea of Richard being feminine.'

'You think it's something bad to be feminine?'

Kate said, 'He never bothered himself all that much over our garden. He was quite happy for our garden just to be just an ordinary suburban garden. I suppose he saved his inspiration for his work; for his intuitions!'

The girl said, 'I think perhaps I should go back to my own room.'

'If we can't talk now, when can we talk? Now's the time to talk, isn't it, traditionally? Après-ski! Did he call it that with you?'

'We must do what is traditional,' the girl said. 'No, never. Après-ski? Never.'

'Suppose he had left me.'

'Après-ski,' the girl said, 'I never heard that.'

'Would you have married him?'

'We never talked about marriage,' the girl said. 'Never.'

'Never? Do you like deceiving people?' Kate said.

'I never deceived anybody,' the girl said. 'Why should I?'

'Don't you sometimes feel it's a thing that makes you feel more alive than anything in the world? To seem to be one thing and actually to be another?'

173

'I was with some friends,' the girl said. 'What do you think I was doing? I went out with some friends.'

'Think of the old,' Kate said, 'what pleasure they get from deception! They make a nurse believe that they've taken their pill and they haven't, that sort of thing gives them more pleasure than any little extra, any Christmas dinner, still to have the power to deceive. Take too good care of them, watch them too carefully and there's nothing for them to do but die. Perhaps that's the final deception. Perhaps even then they watch us, like children pretending to be asleep. It's the last trick they can play on us, isn't it? If he hadn't been married, would he have been the same man, do you think, as far as you were concerned?'

'I didn't give a damn,' the girl said. 'What do you want me to say? Tell me, and I'll say it.'

'Did you never think of me even in the smallest possible way? His wife.'

'I tried not to,' the girl said, 'if you really want to know.'

'In other words, you've answered my question,' Kate said. 'Why did he want you, did you ever wonder that?'

'What are you hoping to find out?'

'I know where I went wrong, of course. I forgot to deceive him. Unless you deceive people there's no distance between you and you can't see them properly. How are we alike, do you think? You and I. Richard told both of us that he loved us. There must be some way.'

'We are alike because he told us that.'

'Did either of us know him or did neither of us know him?'

'Know, know! What is this knowing about? Did we know him, didn't we know him? I don't know, I don't know. I'm tired. Why don't you come to bed?'

'Was he like other men, other men you've known?'

'Like? Like? Like in what way?'

'In bed,' Kate said.

'It's too late,' the girl said. 'Too late for questions.'

Kate said, 'You know, don't you, that I'd do anything you asked me to do, anything in the world, that would please you? Doesn't that give you a nice sense of power?'

'On the contrary,' the girl said, 'on the contrary.'

'I'll even let you use this house if you want to bring people here. If you want to bring that man here for instance, the one you were with tonight. I won't even object to that. I won't object to anything.'

The girl said, 'I don't want anything like that. I wasn't with anyone. What makes you think that's what I want?'

'I'd like to give you everything,' Kate said, 'everything. This house, the car, the boat. I'd like to hand over the whole lot and say "Here you are, it's all yours, the lot, have it, do what you like with it," and then walk out and leave you with everything, just to see what you'd do with it. Just for the hell of it. Just to see what effect it would have on you.'

'I don't want your things.'

'Or I could leave them to you in my will. And you'd have to have them. I could make a will and leave everything to you and then I could start spending all the money. There's another idea. Really nasty! I could buy some poison, some arsenic or something, oh there's probably some weedkiller in the greenhouse, and I could see how long it would take before you decided to kill me. Before you realized that unless you did, it would all be gone. How long before I felt the first little twinge and knew that the doses had started.'

'I don't want to kill you,' the girl said. 'Why would I want to kill you? I don't want your property. I don't want your money.'

'Suppose I did change my will though and then I started to die, to have symptoms. Suppose I did it without your knowing and you were quite innocent. Suppose I even made you go and get my medicine for me, thinking it was my medicine and really it was the poison, so that when the time came there would be your fingerprints on the bottle. Who would believe that you were innocent? Would that policeman to-night believe that you were really devoted to me? And then as I was dying I could think that I was going to be with you as long as you lived. I would be absolutely safe and you'd be unable to revenge yourself on me ever and I'd have all those years to think of you. Or would you walk out when I began to be ill?'

'Do you really hate me that much?'

'*Hate* you? I don't hate you at all. Besides, I'm not going to die of arsenic poisoning just for the pleasure of getting my revenge. No, it was a joke, Mijo, a joke. Can't you take a joke?'

'To say I would leave you! It was you tonight, wasn't it?' the girl said. 'On the landing. There wasn't anybody else, was there?'

44

'You went and slept in my bed,' the girl said.

'You were sleeping so soundly.'

'And left me here. You were here when I went to sleep and then when I woke up, I was alone.'

'I wanted you to sleep soundly.'

'I had such funny dreams, terrible dreams. I don't know what you must have said last night to make me have dreams like the ones I had. Why did you go in my room?'

'I wanted to,' Kate said. 'It was what I wanted all evening. You see how cunning I am when I really want something!'

'Did you sleep well?'

'Like a babe,' Kate said. 'I was a bit silly last night. It must have been the burglar coming back; you're quite wrong, you know, because he certainly did come back. And when I think of what he might have done to you, I feel so guilty I didn't go to the police myself the first time. They might have been able to catch him. Don't ever tell anyone I saw him, will you, by the way, because I dare say it's actually some sort of offence to see a burglar and not report him?'

'My God,' the girl said, 'I'm late. I'm terribly late. I missed my alarm.'

'I'll drive you,' Kate said. 'You go and grab some cornflakes. Meanwhile I'll get the car started. Do you know, I heard the alarm and I was so exhausted, I just turned over and went back to sleep? Will they be terribly upset?'

In the car, the girl said, 'I was never late before. I was maybe ill, but I was never late.'

'Will they be very angry?'

'What does it matter? What does it matter what they are?'

'You think I didn't wake you on purpose. I promise you it's not true.'

'I don't think anything about it,' the girl said. 'I'm late, that's all. And I don't like to be late.'

'And I thought you were the impulsive type,' Kate said. 'I thought you did things on impulse, just when you felt like it. I'll tell you what, I'll cook you a very special supper to make up. Will you be in to supper?'

'I have no plans particularly. Yes, I'll be in.'

'Do you want me to wait and see if everything is all right?'

'There is no problem,' the girl said. 'Of course not. I see you later, yes?'

Kate filled the morning with her purchases. She was planning nothing more than the dinner which she had promised the girl, but she went about the shopping with a sort of casual secrecy. She visited several shops in order to buy the herbs which she could as well have bought in one. She wore her headscarf at some shops and not at others. She put on a coat to go to the butcher; she left it off for the greengrocer. She went to no shop she had patronized before. Once she spoke with an American accent. On another occasion she coughed heavily and managed no more than a husky whisper.

She had not been home long when the telephone

rang. It was a man. He asked for Marie-José. Kate listened to the silence which followed his request.

'Hallo?'

'She's not in at the moment,' Kate said.

'But she does live at this address?'

'Oh yes,' Kate said. 'Who is this speaking, please?'

'My name is Thiviers. Claude Thiviers. I am a friend of Miss Clavand's family. As you may know, it's her birthday on Monday next, and I was afraid that she might be alone. If so, I was hoping I might take her to the theatre, something of that kind.'

'What a kind thought, Mister Thiviers. As a matter of fact, though, I happen to know that she's busy that night. A little celebration, I happened to hear her mention it.'

'I see. Oh that's fine. Is that the lady who lives there?'

'This is Kate Morris speaking, yes. I've heard Marie-José speak of you, of course, Mr Thiviers. I may be a stranger to you, but you're not to me.'

'Ah, yes, well, I was only asking in case she was lonely, you know. Her father and I were at school together. Perhaps when you see her, you will tell her that I telephoned. She – she is all right, I suppose?'

'She is very well indeed, so far as I can tell. I don't think you need to worry about her. She has a lot of friends. She has a nice boy-friend too. She's rarely alone.'

'Will she be in tonight, Mrs Morris?'

'Ah tonight, no,' Kate said. 'Tonight I happen to know she's out.'

'You are very kind.'

'Not at all. Goodbye.'

Kate cooked a duck with olives. She made *pommes*

dauphines and *endives meunière* and a salad. To begin, she was going to grill fresh sardines. For pudding she prepared a *Saint Émilion au chocolat.*

'You're here!' she said, when the girl arrived home, soon after six thirty. 'I was beginning to be afraid you were going to stand me up.'

'My God,' the girl said. 'It's a feast. I can smell. Why should I do that?'

'I owed you something after last night.'

'No, I don't think so at all. On the contrary. Why?'

'Well, after making you late this morning. I want to know what you think of this bread. I went right across London.'

'For bread.'

'When I do something, I like to do it properly. Was there a lot of traffic tonight? See, I even bought candles. I wish it was a little darker. We'll pretend we're in some wonderful little place in Provence, just the two of us, out of season, somewhere a little mysterious, with a sullen chef who absolutely refuses to accept any compliments except a full stomach!'

'Perhaps I should change my clothes,' the girl said.

'Go and put on my Spanish skirt and that orange shirt of mine and I'll lend you some pearls. I've got some pearls that my mother gave me. I never wear them. Go on. Please. And I'll put the sardines on. Five minutes. No longer.'

They drank a Traminer with the sardines; Saint-Amour with the duck. When she saw the *Saint Émilion*, the girl said, 'Oh, God, my favourite, but honestly, darling, it's too much. You know what *gavage* is? You know what that means?'

'Tell me,' Kate said.

'It's when they fatten the geese, you know, in the Périgord. They force-feed them. It's rather horrible actually. They force the corn down their throats with a funnel, the farmers' wives.'

'Oh I know,' Kate said. 'Of course. It's horrible, but the result's so delicious ... *Gavage*, is that what it's called?'

'Yes, *gavage*. Of course, with pigs like me you don't have to do it. At least you don't need a funnel.'

'I was an old-fashioned wife,' Kate said. 'I suppose I should have gone out to work and shown an independent spirit and then I wouldn't have been so vulnerable, but I'll tell you something funny: I always thought I was one of the luckiest women in the world. I thought I had what any woman would want more than anything else. I always used to pity career women. My father told me a story about an uncle of his once. He saw a woman in a bus queue wearing slacks and a man's jacket and tie and he went up to her and gave her a terrific slap on the back and said, "Hullo, Jack old fellow, how are you these days?" I always thought of that woman as a career woman when people talked about career women. I suppose actually she was something else.'

'And they say the English can't cook,' the girl said.

'They also say they can't make love, don't they? Mijo, I want to talk to you seriously.'

'What have I done now?'

'Serious nice not serious nasty. I really and truly don't want to keep this house. I'm not going to stay here.'

'It's such a beautiful house. And what about your son?'

181

'Do you think Bill will ever want to live in this house? I'm not going to stay here. I want to travel. I think we should go to Mexico. If you still want to go.'

'Some day, yes, very much.'

'I'm not saying we should go tonight.'

'My father at the moment is not very well.'

'When did you hear about this?'

'I telephoned. I telephone regularly.'

'We could go all over the world,' Kate said. 'You're really quite a conventional girl, aren't you, in spite of everything?'

'To telephone my father and mother?'

'We have no one to please but ourselves, no other gods. We'd be completely free. Bill doesn't care about me. He's nice to me, he's a nice person, but he doesn't care; he tries to treat me like a real person, but I'm still Mum when it comes to it. You're the only person in the world who really matters to me. You know, there were even parts of Richard I didn't want, parts I didn't want to know about. Parts, even, I didn't like to touch.'

The girl said, 'Perhaps a trip would be a good idea. To get away from this house.'

'Why does one never live as one wants to live?' Kate said. 'More coffee? And we'll drink some port.'

'Who are you trying to get drunk, me or you?'

'Don't you recognize a seduction when you meet one?' Kate said. 'This is a seduction.'

'Are you trying to amuse me, darling? Are you trying to make me laugh, is that what you're trying to do? You don't have to, you know.'

'All these years,' Kate said, 'I've pretended to be something, haven't I? I've pretended to be happy.

I've done my duty. And now I've run out of duties, it's as simple as that. Bill's sixteen. He doesn't need me. He can still use me, but he doesn't want me.'

'You were happy,' the girl said. 'You were.'

'Every week I used to go down to the Citizens' Advice Bureau, you know. I used to give advice.'

'And I'm sure it was very good advice,' the girl said.

'My sweet love, of course it was good advice. It was the best possible advice. I used to listen to those women and they used to tell me their little troubles, about money or about their landlords or their old parents and I gave them the best advice in the world. You see, their problems were to do with bricks and mortar and pounds shillings and pence – pounds and pee, I shall never say that – and I never had those worries. I lived in a different world. I was immortal – I was untouchable. I lived on love. I lived on emotion. We had a joint account. I could draw whatever I needed. I lived on air. I had no problems at all. I would never ever be like them. I've been hateful, haven't I, these last few days, hateful?'

'You sit there,' the girl said, 'and I clear up. You've done enough now. Tonight I do the clearing up.'

'You've worked all day,' Kate said. 'I wanted to give you such a nice evening. Please, I don't want you to do it. "Can't 'elp it." Do you know that song? He loved it. Marlene Dietrich?'

'No, I never heard it. I put the things in the machine,' the girl said, 'how long does that take? I'm not laughing at you. I'm laughing because I love you.'

' "Falling in Love Again", that's what it was called. You find it – you find it so easy to love people, don't you? You don't have to be kind to me, you know, any

more. You don't have to shield me. I'd sooner know
the truth.'

'Truth? What kind of truth?'

'I'll take the New Zealand,' Kate said. 'I'll take the
New Zealand, it's cheaper. How should I know what
kind?'

'You have to make your own truth,' the girl said.
'Isn't that the thing in the end?'

45

'No problem at all,' Kate said, 'what did I tell you? I
said that your father had been taken ill and you had
had to go back to France. They said they were very
sorry to hear it. It looks lovely. I said I'd collect
your cards in the week. It fits you perfectly.'

'It's the most beautiful thing I ever owned. I don't
know how you chose it. It's what I always wanted.
How did you even know that it was my birthday?'

'You told me,' Kate said, 'don't you remember?'

'Never.'

'I asked you, oh a long time ago, when your birthday was and you told me the date. Only because I
wanted to know how old you were. At a time when I
never expected to be giving you a present, let it be
said. Except possibly a dagger between the shoulder
blades. You have very nice shoulder blades. Now we
must get ourselves together or we shall miss the train.'

'I don't remember,' the girl said.

'My sweet, there are so many things you don't remember. Now come on, move!'

They sat silent in the train. There was no one else in the mid-morning compartment. Sun blinded the windows. The girl watched Kate with her heavy, hooded stare. Kate leaned back and closed her eyes under the pressure of her unwavering attention. While she lay there, the girl bent forward and kissed her on the mouth. The rhythm of the train lightened and weighted the kiss. Kate was hypnotized by that soft and furtive regularity. When the girl sat back again, she resumed her unsmiling contemplation of the other woman.

The Alvis had been kept in a garage. Kate had spoken to the man before the weekend and asked him to be sure to have it ready for the road. When he went to start it, the battery was flat. It moaned. The garage was filled with sunshine. The man was made ghostly by the white shafts through the skylight. Kate could find no anger. They would go for a walk, she said, and he could fit a new battery. He could put the old one in the boot.

Kate and the girl walked in the hard street. The garage was opposite the football ground. Double gates were open on to green. A motor mower was at work on the pitch. They walked through to the smell of cut grass. Empty seats rose in shelves behind them. Kate said, 'I love the lines mowers make, don't you? The pattern.'

'It's nice,' the girl said.

'I wonder if that man is going ahead with the development you were working on.'

'Man?'

'Hollis, wasn't that his name? The one you came up to see.'

'Oh, I don't know. Peter would know, I suppose.'

'Yes. I haven't spoken to him for several days. So presumably all's well in that department. At home, I mean. I told you about that. Was it a nice place?'

'Oh boff,' the girl said. 'Yes, it was nice. We were there only an afternoon.'

'And he didn't seem any different from usual, Richard? You had no inkling?'

'He was fine. Very active. Very alive. I told you.'

'No. You told me nothing. Did people know you were lovers?'

'Some people see lovers everywhere, some people never see anything.'

'We used to wonder, he and I, whether people knew. When we first started to sleep together. We used to speculate.'

'We didn't want people to know. Dick anyway.'

'You see that building? That must be the hospital. So you pretended not to be.'

'Not pretended, no. We just kept it to ourselves.'

'That's what people should do,' Kate said. 'You were quite right. Everyone should do that. We should never let it out to anyone. That's where the trouble starts. Perhaps sex should never be talked about. Life should seem to be about something entirely different. That way there would never be any lies, any illusions. Deceptions, oh deceptions everywhere, but no illusions. What do you think? Oh boff, I know! You think I'm just romancing, but I'm not. What do you think about that? A world of silence and terror and nothing else, what do you think?'

'Oh boff – '

'Oh boff, I knew it. I knew it. Mijo, you are funny.'

'Perhaps not all that funny always,' the girl said.

'Now the sun's gone in,' Kate said. 'My, it's turned chilly suddenly! What really attracted you to him? What made you want Richard particularly?'

'Oh la,' the girl said. 'Not again.'

'I'd like the truth.'

'What did I say last time? He was an attractive man, I worked with him, I liked him, he liked me. What am I to say? He admired me, he wanted me, he was unhappy.'

'Happy birthday, Mijo,' Kate said, 'happy birthday. Let's go and see if the old Alvis is back in commission. It's getting late. Clever girl you are! We shall miss our lunch.'

'We find a sandwich,' the girl said. 'Why clever?'

'We find nothing of the sort. Because you are. I've planned this outing, you don't seem to realize; I've gone to a lot of trouble. It's all planned to the last iota. The place we're going is really rather special. I think you'll like it. The proprietor's a real character.'

The restaurant was in an old mill. The owner was renowned for his temper. He had once refused to serve a couple who arrived five minutes late, as a result of fog, after driving over fifty miles. The stories of his disagreeable nature enhanced his success. People thought themselves privileged when he failed to abuse them. Kate had first visited the place with her father and mother. Mr Sells had kept his boat not far from the mill. This time, she had booked a one-thirty table. When the Alvis drew up outside, the proprietor came running out of the door. He kissed Kate's hand and she smiled at the tickle of his moustache. He made Mijo a speech in effusive Belgian French. Everything was ready. The ladies could eat as soon as they wished. *'Toujours on fait son meilleur pour les jolies femmes!'*

'Gavage,' Kate said. 'Wasn't that the expression?'

The first course was trout in aspic.

The girl said, 'Darling, I have to talk to you.'

Kate said, 'It was funny to be in the old Alvis again. The miles we've done in that car. The miles you've done.'

'I'm worried about you, darling.'

'I think you should get out more,' Kate said. 'I quite agree: I've been very selfish.'

'You should see other people,' the girl said. 'You see nobody. It's my fault. When I'm in the house, you never see anyone, you never invite anyone. It's not right.'

'That dress looks so lovely,' Kate said.

'Bill will soon be home for his holidays. What happens then?'

'He's going to camp for the first week and then ... Well, he's got his friends; I expect they've got their own plans.'

'I can't stay in the house,' the girl said. 'Obviously I can't.'

'And how are the ladies getting on, is everything as it should be?'

'Delicious trout,' Kate said. 'Just perfection. But then it always is.'

'And the birthday lady?'

The girl looked at the proprietor and nodded, once.

'*Très, très bien. Très bien.* So – it is a long time since we have seen you.'

'Yes, alas,' Kate said.

'You are on holiday in England?'

The girl shook her head, once.

'*Très bien, très très bien. Alors,* well, I leave you to enjoy yourselves, I hope! *Bon appétit, bon appétit.*'

The main course was stuffed quails.

'That man is really a fool,' the girl said. 'He is really a fool.'

'You want to leave me,' Kate said.

'I hate that kind of man,' the girl said.

Kate said, 'And Mexico? He's a character. He does no harm. What about our trip to Mexico?'

'He is a fraud, a fake,' the girl said. 'He is ridiculous. All that nonsense.'

'He's a good cook.'

'But all this bowing and all the compliments and the malice behind them. I can't stand that kind of thing.'

'Answer me,' Kate said.

'I have to see how my father is.'

'You said yourself it was nothing to worry about. Think of those beaches. Empty beaches. And the sun. The Caribbean. You can swim naked, there are so few people.'

'Oh la,' the girl said. 'You've been reading.'

'There is someone, isn't there?' Kate said. 'It's nothing to do with your father.'

'He is ill,' the girl said. 'You know he is.'

'Why do you lie?'

'You think I don't want to go to Mexico? Of course I do.'

'A little cheese for the ladies.'

'Cheese, Mijo?'

'No thank you, darling. No cheese.'

'Pas de fromage pour mademoiselle?'

'No cheese. Coffee.'

'A *Méringue Chantilly* perhaps. *Specialité de la Maison.* Or we have some *petits pots, vanille, chocolat . . .'*

'Coffee.'

'We'll just have some coffee, Mr Palanquin, thank you.'

'The moustache. The hands all like this. He is the sort of man who occurs only in the farces of Feydeau and the French restaurants of England. What an idiot, I must say!'

'I know he exists,' Kate said.

'Oh God, Kate, please.'

'Or are you a fraud as well? Because I know he does.'

The waiter was scarcely fourteen. He did not have to shave, but his old face was creased with apprehension. He brought them unspilt coffee in shaking, watched hands. The girl gave him a sudden smile and he was rattled. He put down the cups and waited.

Kate said, 'I'm right, aren't I?'

The girl said, 'Darling, I never apologize. I never apologize, I never make confessions. So.'

'You like to be cruel,' Kate said. 'You like to create a situation where people don't know what's true and what's false. What's actually wrong with your father? Come on. Anything?'

'People telephone the house,' the girl said, 'and you don't pass on the messages. Isn't that true? He is a bully, that man. You see him with the boy? I hate that sort of man.'

'Oh men,' Kate said. 'It's Josh, I presume. That American with the awful breath.'

'Sometimes I understand exactly how you must have been with him. You always pretend to do things only because other people want to do them. But that is exactly what you want, what other people want, to have them hot and you stay cold.'

Kate said, 'I know what you're saying is supposed to be nasty, but I don't know what it's supposed to mean.'

'Like the other night. You trapped him and now you try to trap me.'

'Is that what he told you?'

'It's what you did, my darling. Let's not be silly. Why do you think he had girls?'

46

'You know,' Kate said, 'I don't remember any of this road. I drove all the way up and all the way back and I don't remember any of it. Of course, we've cut off one bit, going for lunch, but we've been back on it for several miles now and I could swear I'd never been on it before in my life. I know you were being deliberately cruel at lunch, what you said. I'm sorry if I provoked you. It wasn't intentional.'

They had joined the main road below where they had exploded the oak. More work was being done on another section. Hedges were being rooted out and flung on fires. The landscape was choked with low smoke, the colour of dead herring. Surveyors had marked the path of the second lane with wooden crosses. It passed through gardens and close to brick houses. Bulldozers had razed a brown track. Shrubs and uprooted flowers were piled on the verges. Several of the houses had been abandoned. They were so close to the new highway that no one could live there. Even though they looked habitable, they would have to be destroyed. It was a relief to finish the miles where work was in progress and to come on to a broad section of completed dual carriageway. The smoke thinned and cleared. The road was clean and fast. There was no sign of private garden or private house. The road ran straight along the railway. A train came on stilted wheels and went by like a toy.

'You didn't mean girls,' Kate said. 'If you want to leave me, you can always leave without telling lies or being deliberately hurtful. If I hurt you, I'm sorry, but you don't have to reply in kind, certainly not with lies. You obviously never believed it, I can see that, but we were happy. Just because you want to leave, you don't have to take all my confidence with you. I thought we were past that stage.'

'I can see why he was afraid of you,' the girl said.

They overtook lorry after lorry, each with a container chained to it. One of them was refrigerated. The casing of the cooling system was flapping with the speed.

'I wonder if he knows,' Kate said. 'If that came off, it could be dangerous. You think he was afraid of me, do you?'

'Of course.'

'Am I so frightening?'

'It's too late to matter now.'

'We are hurt!' Kate said. 'And I thought you were the strong one.'

'He was afraid to talk to you,' the girl said.

'I'm ashamed of him sometimes, I really am, because he must have told you the first thing that came into his head.'

'He did.'

'We talked all the time. We were never in any sort of difficulty about having things to talk about. I loved to talk to him. Did he give you the impression that we sat and looked dolefully at each other in the evenings and couldn't think of anything to say? That was very naughty, because I promise you we didn't. You know, I'm sure that thing is going to fall off. You turn round and look and see if you don't think so too. I wonder whether I shouldn't tell somebody.'

The girl said, 'He was always going to talk to you, but he never did.'

'Always going to talk to me but he never did! You'll have to explain, I'm afraid. I've lost you.'

'It doesn't matter.'

'There you go being naughty, being deliberate again. You know I can't stand it when you do that.'

'He married you because he was afraid of you and he stayed with you because he was afraid of you. O.K.?'

'You seriously believe that, do you? After all the talks we've had? When you've admitted yourself . . . '

'O.K., forget it. I'm sorry. Forget it.'

'It's beyond apologies. This time, Mijo, it really is beyond apologies.'

'Then put me down. Put me down at the round-about, O.K.?'

'O.K., O.K., everything's O.K. suddenly, but it's not O.K. at all. It's far from O.K. He married me because he was afraid of me, you said. He may have told you that. Men will say anything to get a girl into bed, or excuse themselves for having done it and then wanting to keep it quiet.'

'He didn't want his parents to know, right? And you blamed him because he hurt you one time. Well, as far as I am concerned, men don't have to excuse themselves for wanting to go to bed with me.'

'I don't imagine they have much need.'

'You are really a very vulgar woman, Kate. I hope you don't mind if I say that.'

'I take it as a compliment. I'm sure it was intended as a compliment. Oh darling ... you might at least have a sense of humour.'

'You did him a favour. You do everyone favours. He was the bad one. He took you to bed. For that he owed you something. His life. You said to him after that first time, do you remember, "As far as I am concerned, we're married –" '

'He said that,' Kate said. 'He was the one who said that. And he told you – you're lying. You're lying. Why are you?'

'I am not lying.'

'I never made him do anything. I never wanted him to do anything he didn't want to do. God, I wish he was here. Oh God, I wish he was. You think I – I hooked him, is that what you're trying to say, that I got my hooks into him and wouldn't let him go?'

'Would you ever have let him go? You know you wouldn't.'

'He didn't want to go,' Kate said. 'What do you mean, go?'

The new road had ended. They avoided a town and went over the railway and then on to an older section of dual carriageway where chestnut trees had been allowed to live. A long brick wall protected the grounds of a mansion.

'O.K.,' the girl said.

'And you can say what you like.'

'O.K.,' the girl said.

The traffic slowed. Drivers in the outside lane began to look back and wink to go left. It was impossible to see anything wrong with the outside lane, but it was closed by plastic witches' hats.

Kate said, 'I would have known.'

'Darling,' the girl said, 'he was dying to go.' She turned to look at a surveyor and his clerk who were lining up in a field.

'All husbands have times when they say things,' Kate said. 'And of course it's perfectly natural that you should try and push all the guilt on to me.'

'I don't have any guilt,' the girl said. 'I meant you no harm; I did you no harm.'

'I wasn't thinking of me,' Kate said.

47

'Until a minute ago,' the girl said, 'I still loved you. Now it's finished.'

'I'm going to stop for petrol.'

'Now it's finished. Up until a minute ago, I believed that you were honestly in need of someone, even of me. Now I feel disgusted. You disgust me. I see now what you've been doing to me. The other night, when you made love to me, that was not love. You were searching me. I can feel your tongue on me now and it's disgusting. It was the tongue of a detective. Your tongue in me was the tongue of a detective. Your fingers, your fingers were the fingers of a *douanier*. You were looking for something. No wonder you wouldn't take off your clothes. You had to be cool, didn't you? You couldn't become emotionally involved.'

'Eight super please, and I'd like the stamps. Mrs Jenkins collects the stamps.'

'Damn Mrs Jenkins,' the girl said. 'You hate her. Why do you give her things?'

'You liked it at the time. Have you forgotten? But then of course you find it easy to forget, don't you? As for instance you forget that if it hadn't been for you, my husband would be alive today. Richard would be alive today. Thank you. Oh and you're giving tokens I see. What are they for exactly?'

'Four tokens and you get a bottle of these spices they're giving away.'

'Oh what a good idea! I'll take those as well then. Or have I got enough for one already?'

'You have actually. Eight gallons. They're inside if you want to choose.'

'What a good idea, trying to raise the standard of English cooking. I'll tell you what, you choose for me, would you do that?'

The girl clapped her hands together, once, twice, three times. '*Le flegme Anglais*. Bravo, bravo.'

'You dare to judge me, my sweet, do you? You actually have the nerve to do that. When if it weren't for you, he'd be alive. He'd be alive today.'

'If it weren't for me, did you say?'

'Celery salt,' Kate said, 'that's a very good choice. Thank you so much, I shall treasure that. I didn't kill him. I didn't go and desert him – '

'Perhaps that was his greatest misfortune.'

'I'd like to crash this car,' Kate said. 'I'd like to crash this car and I'm quite capable of doing it, so be careful.'

'You were the killer,' the girl said. 'If you want to crash, crash. You don't frighten me.'

'Everyone has quarrels,' Kate said. 'And that's always what they tell other people about. Men never tell anyone how happy they've been.'

'For instance that holiday in the Dordogne.'

'Days and days on our own.'

'The best times you ever had together,' the girl said. 'Sex twice and three times a day.'

'Yes, it was – it was – '

'During that time,' the girl said, 'he was in love with a woman who lived near Saffron Walden. A Mrs somebody. She had to go to South Africa. He took you to France.'

'Mijo, I still love you. I love your innocence. I love your malice even. You're like a little cat.'

'He wanted to be free, but you'd never let go. You tore him in half. He was afraid of what you would do. He knew how passionate you could be.'

'I thought a minute ago I was cold.'

'Passionate to keep things as they were,' the girl said.

'And you seriously and truly believe that he'd leave everything he cared for in order to go off with someone like you?'

'With me,' the girl said. 'With me. Not someone like me. Me. You want us both to be on the same side, you and I, you want us both to be victims, but that's where you are wrong. We're not on the same side. We are not fellow victims. I don't hate him.'

48

'You know what we could do. We could stop at a delicatessen and buy something for supper. Something simple. Perhaps some of that Danish caviare, it's not expensive and it's not bad either. There's nothing much this side of London, funnily enough, but once we get through the West End there are several quite decent places. There's one in Earl's Court we used to go to.'

The girl said, 'Don't bother.'

'It's not a question of bother. Lunch is a long time ago. That awful man, wasn't he absurd? I agree with you, he was absolutely absurd. To a Frenchwoman particularly he must seem completely inane. You know what I'm thinking of doing? I'm thinking seriously of going into some sort of business.'

'Good idea,' the girl said. 'You should.'

'The trouble with any kind of food place is that it's such a tie. It ties one dreadfully. Of course if one can get reasonable help, it makes a difference. There's a glut in London at the moment; but the country's another thing. I don't cook badly – '

'You cook very well,' the girl said. 'God.'

'Well, thank you, a civil word at last. Thank you. When we used to go down to see Bill we could never find anywhere decent to eat, not within miles. We used to have these appalling set meals in country inns, plastic chicken and two veg. We'd try one after another. Somewhere in that area could do very well indeed. Simple, tasty cooking, with a touch of the French provincial, nothing ambitious and absolutely no hand-kissing, what do you think?'

'Very possibly,' the girl said.

'And you could design the place,' Kate said. 'I'd give you your head. You could do whatever you wanted, within a budget, of course. You'd have to keep your head in a budget! Do you think you could manage to do that? Do you think you could avoid going mad?'

'I really don't know,' the girl said.

'You'll have to do better than that,' Kate said. 'There's a delicatessen that doesn't look too curled at the edges. Shall we see what they've got?'

'I'm going out tonight, Kate,' the girl said.

'You're going out? You never said.'

'I'm going out,' the girl said.

'Well, well, well, when was this arranged?'

'It's my birthday,' the girl said.

'And happy birthday to you,' Kate said. 'Happy very birthday to you indeed. Well, well, well. Aren't you a sly Miss? You are a sly Miss! Or did you tell me and I never heard you? What's the story this time?'

'You said we would have the day together and so naturally, I assumed – '

'A perfectly natural assumption. The day is the day and the night is the night.'

'I do have friends,' the girl said.

'Variety, variety,' Kate said. 'You're so right. So all this was arranged in advance, was it? Regardless of how the day worked out. You're not doing anything so crude, I mean to say, as paying me out for giving you such a horrible day?'

'It wasn't horrible,' the girl said.

'It was O.K., am I right? It was O.K. as O.K. can be. Well, I'm glad to hear it. Some friends, eh, or is it a friend? Mijo, look at me, my sweet, you might at least look at me, because it's polite to look at people. Oh my, what a face! Is it the same man?'

The girl said, 'That's my business, isn't it?'

'Ah well, that's a sacrifice I'm used to having to make. Whenever he used to tell me that he had business, I never questioned it. I never doubted it. It's a principle of mine never to be jealous where business is involved.'

'I never wanted to hurt you. I thought I could avoid it. I see I was wrong.'

'No, no, I beg to differ. I appreciate how kind you're being, letting me into your business secrets, sharing intimate things of that kind. I call that really royal, such frankness, such lack of shame. Who is he?'

'A man, a man.'

'Or a boy, is it a boy this time? I saw you with that waiter at lunch.'

'I beg your pardon?'

'Fourteen years old, if that. He blushed when you looked at him.'

'What waiter?'

'Who brought us the coffee. You looked at him, you teased him, you wanted to excite him, just for the fun of it. I saw you. Don't say anything, because I saw you. Or is this one married, like someone else I could mention? Is there that kind of fun attached to this one as well? Or is he one of those beautiful cads girls like you always lose their hearts to, one of those ones who wears a gold chain round their wrists and round their whatsits too for all I know?'

The girl sat like a hitch-hiker and looked round the car.

'Never mind, it's one more, I suppose, to give your famous smile to. Another one to call darling. Another one to make a fool of yourself over. Another one to say deeper to and ah and yes, another one to hurt when you've had enough of him. Another one to leave in the ditch. Ah, I'm right, am I?'

'Right? About what?'

'I saw that little smile. I saw it all right. Was I right? Is he one of those long-haired types who spends all his time looking in the mirror and only wants you to do things to him? Is he one of those? Or is it something deeper, something more serious, something I could never understand?'

'What was her name did you say? Erica?'

49

'I won't let you go.'

'Kate, I'm going.'

'I won't. I won't. You can do anything you like.'

'Believe me, darling – '

'No. You said you hated me. All right, you hate me. I deserve it.'

'Darling . . .'

'Don't call me darling. Unless you want to hurt me. If you want to, do it. But at least know what you're doing.'

'I am leaving this house. I must. My father is ill. Please let go of me now.'

'Not tonight,' Kate said. 'I took so much trouble over today. I know it went wrong, I know you didn't enjoy it, but at least realize how much trouble I took over it. Please come back tonight. Bring him back if you want to. You can have my room. You can have the big bed. If you don't come back tonight, I shall kill myself.'

'Kate, my father is ill. Do you think I would have left my job if I had meant to stay? I have to go back to France. They need me there. Tonight is nothing.'

'I need you,' Kate said. 'Without you I shan't be able to live. I mean it quite literally. I'll be the housekeeper. I'm quite happy just to be the house-keeper. I'll look after you. You can do exactly as you please. Don't go.'

'Darling, do you think I could bring myself to humiliate you that much?'

'But I'm asking you to do it. I'm asking you.'

'I could never stay. In your heart you know it.'

'You want a man. You hypocrite. You hypocrite. Admit you're a hypocrite. I'm not the first woman you've corrupted. Admit it. Am I? I'm not the first and I won't be the last. It amuses you, this kind of thing.'

'No, it does not amuse me in the least. I no longer love you and nor do you me, that is what is corrupt. That is corrupt.'

'As you said so kindly before. I have made a note of it.'

'But I do care for you. I care enough to know that I must leave tonight.'

'Are you going to carry a bag around with you all evening? Are you going to take your plastic bag to Annabel's or the Savoy Grill or wherever Bubbles decides to take you?'

'I'll leave my things if it gives you any pleasure.'

'You'll take them with you. Every last filthy article. I'm not having you leave things in my house. If you go, you can take your belongings. And your pills, you mustn't forget your pills. We don't want an accident. If you go, you damned well take your things. That's the least you can do, and the least, I have no doubt, is exactly what you will do.'

'Darling, try to forgive me, try to understand. Don't cry.'

'I'm not crying.'

'Because you knew all along. Admit it. Admit it.'

'I was a fool, I admit that. But then I was always a fool. I don't suppose I shall change now. The only change I shall see now . . . You're right to go. In your

203

position I'd go as well. Never imagine that I blame you. I hate you, but I don't blame you.'

'Call your son. Talk to him. He is a nice boy. Talk to him. The young understand more than you think.'

'Why couldn't you have waited a year or two,' Kate said, 'and had him? And kept it in the family!'

'Kate, I'm going now.'

'You made love in the car as well, I suppose, didn't you? Please tell me the truth.'

'Once or twice.'

'When we were lovers, we had no car. People didn't. We did it once standing up. In Richmond Park. I never even knew you could. Standing up.'

'There are – '

'So many ways, aren't there? I say, I do wonder if I shall ever have another man.'

'I'm sorry I made you unhappy.'

'On the contrary,' Kate said, 'on the contrary. Have you my key?'

'We pretended it was the same man we loved, but it never was the same man. He was as different as you and I are different. And you and I are very different.'

'You're right, you're right, you're absolutely right. I do so agree.'

'Suppose I described the man I loved and you described him and we compared the descriptions.'

'It's true,' Kate said, 'I don't dispute it for a moment. My key, do you have it?'

'I'm going to be late,' the girl said.

'I'm so sorry', Kate said, 'that I haven't a dagger, that I can't do what a man would do.'

'Find love,' the girl said. 'I hope you do.'

'Oh I shall,' Kate said. 'Underground with the Oriole.'

50

She was impatient for the girl to be gone. The bicycle ticked as she walked away. As soon as the street was silent, Kate went for her coat and her driving gloves. She took an old pair of pyjama trousers from the boots cupboard and stuffed it in her pocket. Then she went out and locked the door behind her. She drove the Alvis into Richmond Park and stopped at a picnic site. The last of the London commuters were coming through. They watched the deer and the deer watched them.

She took the petrol cap off the tank and fed the twisted end of the pyjama leg into the tank. When the whole leg was soaked with petrol, she pulled it out and pushed it back until there was a wet part protruding from the tank. Then she took Richard's college lighter from her bag. She saw the celery salt on the back shelf. She retrieved it and put it in her bag. Then she held the flame under the pyjama cord where she had tied it round the leg. When it was smouldering, she turned and walked away from the car.

The explosion surprised her. It was fiercer than she had expected. She was some distance away, but she felt the heat blowing towards her. She had parked the car several yards away from the traffic, by the benches and the bins with their brown paper bags for rubbish. The first few cars went on by, but soon someone stopped. He had an extinguisher and worked on the flames. Kate was walking down towards the gate by that time.

She might have been returning from work. There was new energy in her movements. She unlocked the front door and went into the hall. She did not close it behind her. She could have been leaving it open for some packages she was going back for in a minute. There was a breeze blowing. A bill slid from the lop-sided table. Kate went into the sitting-room and waited for some time. Then she went into the kitchen and opened the back door. She turned on the low lights over the sink. She lit no other light. She walked from room to room. In each one, she unlocked the windows and opened them to their widest limit. The breeze was enough to stir the curtains. She propped the front door with the claw for removing boots which her mother had given them one Christmas. The breeze moved into the house like the first gentle waters of a flood. She went upstairs and took off her clothes and lay naked on her bed in the darkness listening to the furtive lap of the breeze as it sipped at the house.

51

No one will come. In a few hours it will be dark and cold. I shall doze and I shall wake up and I shall be cold. No one will come. I shall get up and put on my dressing-gown. I shall no longer be naked but I will still be cold. I will go downstairs and I will shut the doors and the windows. I will put the bolt across the doors. I shall turn on a light and I shall recoil from the glare as if someone had touched me. No one will have touched me. I shall have a drink, which I shall not finish, and I will shudder. I will run a hot bath. I shall be cold even in the heat, but only for a time. I shall feel warmer. I shall cry. I shall stop crying. I will dry myself and I will powder myself and I will go to bed properly. I shall sleep. In the morning, it will be morning. She will not come back. I will pretend that I am not thinking of her. Tonight and tomorrow I shall think of her as she was under my lips. I shall think of physical things for many days, perhaps for weeks. I shall greet the postman when he brings me registered correspondence from my solicitor and I shall smile at the milkman, who always reads my notes. They will not think that I dream of them being cruel men who might take me without a word and against my will. I shall think of such things only for a while. I shall read magazines. I will no longer have desires. I shall have dreams but I will not remember the dreams. I will distil nothing from them. I shall think of Mijo from time to time, but I shall cease to think of her under my lips. I shall cease to imagine her flesh. I shall remember that I cared for her and that I still care for her although she has left me. I shall remember that I hate her. She will not write. One day she will come to the house. She will ring the bell and my mouth will turn down slightly when I see her. I shall not reproach her and I shall not question her. I will suggest, perhaps, that she let me have the child and that she leave it with me. She will shake her head. She will go to an address I will find for her and all will be well. Afterwards she will stay with me for a few days. Bill will be at Cambridge. He will come home and he will meet her and he will say, yes, he remembers her vaguely. He will have a girl, a girl who sits politely with us and then whispers that it is time that they were going. Mijo will stay a day longer than she said, and then she will go. She will kiss me on either cheek and she will give me, on the doorstep, at the last moment, a smile that promises she has not forgotten. I will not reply to that smile. I will promise that I have forgotten and that will make her happy. She will hold my hand and when she is back wherever she is going, she will write to me. She will say that she will always love me for understanding her and for helping her. I will smile then, and the lines will stay on my face. She will not reply to my reply, except that a card will come from her, from an exotic place, many weeks later. I shall dress carefully, better than before, but without ostentation. No one except the doctor will ever see my breasts again. I shall have my hair done once a week as usual, but I shall no longer go into town. I shall find a local man who will do perfectly well at a fraction of the cost. I shall begin to be anxious about money. My solicitor will assure me that I have nothing to worry about. I shall not allow his kindness to deprive me of my little worries. I shall join some committees. I shall be very reliable. My pleasure will come from conforming to what people believe me to be. I shall never be suspected of being anything other than I appear and I shall appear to be exactly what I am: an older woman.